THE HOMECOMING

James H Ward

The Homecoming

Published by Howard J Shedden

Gauteng, South Africa

vumbrimu@gmail.com

ISBN 978-0-620-83360-8

Cover illustration and design by Trisha Lee Nuttall

Layout and publication facilitation by Boutique Books

Chapter 1

It was the days that were the worst. Always the days that dragged slowly to an end. In the first week she had already cleaned everything that could be cleaned. She had washed all the sheets and remade the beds, but they remained unused. Freshly laundered clothes stayed neatly folded in cupboards, unworn, and towels hung on their rails or lay folded in closets, fragrantly awaiting noisy bath times. The bathrooms were spotlessly clean too. Windows around the house had been cleaned inside and out. Everything was put away in the kitchen and even the work tops were spotless. She was so bored that she had polished the kettle, the toaster and even scoured all the pots with Handy Andy. When Melanie was home she was never allowed to scour the pots, but she loved doing it. It was easier than using water and sand, like they used to do at home, and it made a nice smell.

The dogs followed her around, unusually subdued, and waited patiently for their meals, every morning and evening. They went to their usual places and wolfed down their food, and were even beginning to watch her face and listen to her gentle instructions: 'Sit boy, sit now, you must be a good boy'. They sensed the emptiness together and no longer barked at her. They roamed uneasily around the empty house, shadowing her movements from room to room, lying and watching her with their strange, golden eyes. As the evening light closed in on the house they would sit on the stoep and gaze into the distance as if suddenly remembering something that had happened to someone very far away and long ago.

Every time she moved between the rooms she was accompanied by the sound of them following her, their worn claws and big paws on hard floors, and was aware of dogs' tails beating on carpets and striking the furniture as a brown tide of lonely animals flowed behind her and settled around her feet.

It was so quiet.

The days were the loneliest times. No little one to push in the pram until he slept. No nappies to be changed. No boy to bath and wash. No little girl to welcome home from school and help change into play clothes. Just quiet, and quiet followed by more quiet, except for the continuous sound of cicadas outside. The money they paid was much more than usual, but she hadn't realised what it would feel like, looking after an empty house. Sometimes tears would suddenly fill her eyes. Things happened that were unexpected and she didn't know what to do. The gardener told her that the lawnmower needed more fuel and there was none left, but she didn't know where to get more, or what kind to buy. He spoke angrily towards her, as though it were her fault.

Khanyi had spoken to them three times while they were overseas. Once they had phoned from his brother's house, once from their friends' house and once from somewhere else, she thought they said France. They sounded so far away and the children's voices on the phone were different. She didn't know if France was the same as England but on the phone it sounded different. Once they called late at night while she was asleep. She told them the dogs looked cold so she'd made them a fire to keep warm. They'd laughed when she said this and she didn't understand why. Each day she would go to the study, full of so many books, papers and files that she longed to stack up in neat piles but had to leave alone, and take up a red pen and draw a line through another day on the calendar. Slowly, slowly the number of remaining days grew less.

The evenings and nights were better. She would wrap herself in a blanket and sit on the couch in the lounge, with all the dogs around her lying, kicking and dreaming. She could switch on the TV, drink some tea and then go to sleep. Time passed more quickly at night.

She didn't like the films full of shouting, swearing and fighting, and with scenes of men beating women or hurting each other, or of children crying. How was this something to watch and enjoy? She sometimes watched news, but it upset her when it showed hungry, dirty children covered with flies, even hungrier than the poorest Shangaan families at home. She was scared by scenes of men beating up women.

She liked the gospel singing and the choirs – she knew many of the songs and could sing with them – and liked hearing the local preachers hoarsely bellowing at their followers to repent, and to watch them casting out demons. Best of all were the local shows from the rural areas. Often she thought she saw people she knew, one of her brother's small father's sisters, or one of her other sisters from her step-mother's family. She loved the soap operas but was shocked at the way whites behaved, especially in America. The one called Leo was married to the lady with red hair but was also sleeping with her sister, then last week he was also kissing with another man called Towers! It was very confusing. She was glad her work family was nothing like this. She feared to use the phone too much, knowing it was expensive to talk for long, but often wished her friends would call her more. It always stopped working when there was thunder, but at other times it worked.

One day something happened to the alarm clock. The radio began playing by itself and she could not close it off. She was scared of breaking something. She turned it softer, but it was still whispering all the time. When they phoned the next time she asked what to do and the Mnumzane said just pull out the plug. Now it was quiet again. She couldn't work out how to play the radio from the hifi – there were too many switches – but she could play the small one in the kitchen and had tuned it to her favourite channel Ukhozi FM, where the handsome guys with deep voices spoke perfect Zulu very quickly, and chatted up women callers so eloquently. It was too nice, that one.

After the house had been cleaned, Khanyisile had rubbed wood oil into the old furniture and polished the ancient pieces, watered the plants, fed the dogs, washed their bowls and answered the phone to write down messages. Because of the business there were many calls for Mr. Barton. The little pile of notes in her neat handwriting was growing.

She would sometimes walk to the post office and collect the mail. There was still money in the drawer for bread and milk, and some left for meat, and she would walk to the store and buy this every few days. She would not tell anyone that she was alone in the house because she knew it was best not said. When one of her uncles, the driver of a bread truck, stopped to greet her and asked where the boss was, it was better to say they went to Durban and were coming back soon. But the days seemed long and the nights were becoming cold and the house stood empty and unfulfilled.

Soon, the wall calendar with its pictures of old castles in the snow showed that the last week had started. She kept checking it and started feeling excited, knowing that the special day was coming close. That Friday with a red circle was getting near at last.

On the 14th of August, they would come that night from Jo'burg together in the big car, all suitcases and noise and hugging and it would be busy again. Her family would be returning. If she were at her rural home, they would ring bells, brew five day beer and definitely slaughter a goat.

Just five days left.

Her little girl Jackie would be so talkative, telling her everything at once, and the little boy would be smothering her with kisses, whispering secrets in her ear in his own language and clinging to her neck, not letting go. They would be noisy and excited and talk to her without stopping, breathlessly telling her all about what things they had seen and showing their new clothes and what they did at granddad's house and what they had to eat on the plane. They had become like her children too.

Last time they travelled far, to another country, they'd brought her back a special suitcase, red in colour, with cloth inside and even having inside pockets. A high quality suitcase you would never find here, and inside were chocolates and some new clothes of a type she had never seen. It was the finest present she had ever been given, and she had cried when she received it. When she was small, once or twice at Christmas she had been allowed to eat KFC at home with the other children, but only if her father had not been drinking. She had never been given a present all of her own to keep, even on her birthday. The Bartons were kind people and they never allowed the children to disrespect her. If it was her birthday or Christmas they would always buy her real presents. They were unlike the cruel woman from Bloemfontein who used to ration her bread and tea.

Only five more days. She would call the dogs at supper and talk to them like they were children at school. 'Dogs, *five* more days then they are going to be *home!*' but they just looked at her as if trying to understand, ears lifted but still confused. The days dragged and passed slowly by.

Chapter 2

On the day before they were due to come home, she was startled just after dawn by birds screaming loudly in the trees outside. It sounded like the warning noises that lowveld birds make when there is a green mamba in the branches or on the ground beneath, but the dogs were still quiet.

She unlocked the door and slowly edged her way into the cool garden, sensing something harmful in the fresh scented air, and strangely fearful of what might be outside. She walked warily towards the source of the sound and began peering into the lower branches of the big Mkuhlwa tree, her eyes adjusting to the patches of light. Some unseen corruption had changed the air around her, bringing with it a strange sense of evil, floating somewhere above the grass.

She could sense from where the noise was loudest that there was something there, something that seemed aware of her, but she couldn't see it properly. She walked slowly around, peering nervously into the gloomy branches of the huge tree, and the screeching seemed to quieten around her, as though the wild birds sensed they had an ally.

She began to make out something pale and motionless in the mottled light, her view obscured by the foliage and branches.

Taking a few more steps closer for a clearer view, she realised to her absolute terror that a large owl was above her. It was creamy coloured, speckled on its chest and as big as a five kilogram bag of mealie meal, perched utterly motionless on a branch, with both eyes firmly closed, impervious to the darting birds swooping down on it and screaming continuously.

It was the biggest owl she had ever seen. It was an ominous, silent presence, seemingly unconcerned at the panic it was causing.

The dogs had heard the door opening and followed her out into the garden. They sniffed deeply and gazed into the cool emptiness, and occasionally one would freeze and stare intently at things only they could feel or sense in the distance. The female, intensely protective over Khanyi and their surrounding plot of land, growled softly, her hackles rising, but there was nothing else there. She suddenly felt a deep sense of unease.

Khanyi was deeply terrified and began trembling. Her skin grew cold. The atmosphere had changed and had suddenly grown chill. Only harm would come from this event.

She thought of the time when she was about nine, walking home from school with her classmates, dragging a long stick with one yellow and one vivid red leaf impaled on it, singing and skipping, their bare dusty feet burning from the heat of the gravel road. On that day, she saw an owl suddenly swoop silently right over their heads, across their path and alight in a tree. It turned its head in that sinister way and gazed silently at them, slowly blinking. The head moved round like a chameleon's eyeball.

She had felt that same sudden cooling of the air, a peculiar stillness and the presence of something very dark. The following day she had been bluntly told that her mother was late. She had been taken to a local clinic and had died there, still waiting for treatment, dying from an ailment that was never explained to them as children. They only said she got a stomach sickness.

She had died from stomach sickness.

Barely six years later, she had gone through the shame of a schoolgirl pregnancy and the pain of childbirth while still a child herself, without sympathy from any quarter and without her own mother. She gave birth to a child, and she'd raised and would try to breast feed her baby at sixteen, with no one to show her how. Her father took a new wife soon after the funeral, as there were many children and grandchildren needing care, but the new wife hated her, and hated the baby, naming her Mafikizolo, the one who came yesterday. Khanyi never had a say in the naming of her own child.

The owl in the garden was going to bring evil into her life again.

That night, instead of being excited about tomorrow's homecoming she slept fitfully, disturbed by her saddest memories and secret sorrows. She desperately wanted a man but viewed them all with deep suspicion, having been warned by her pastor of the Independent African Methodist Church of Zion that they all wanted her for sex. She was scared to talk to any young men, fearful that they might do to her what had happened before. She was a beautiful young woman in the prime of her life, but such vain thoughts hardly occurred to her. She thought herself dirty, sullied, like spoilt goods, because that was what she had been told at church, time and time again, to remind her of her sin. Her purity was lost forever, they had told her.

Chapter 3

THE LONG AWAITED MORNING FINALLY broke brightly across the skies and she went around the house double checking everything she had checked before. She laid a fire for their return, and thawed the last of the meat, planning to prepare food for them in the afternoon.

She broke off a small branch with strong leaves and many twigs to use as a broom, and swept the driveway of twigs and leaves, and even washed the smallest dog, which tried to bite her.

She changed into her Sunday two piece outfit to greet them, and sat and waited patiently all afternoon, her hands neatly folded in her lap.

Two times, she clearly heard the sound of a car's engine in the distance. The second time it grew louder and her heart lifted and began racing and she started walking quickly down the driveway towards the noise, smiling and wanting to get a better view of the first open piece of gravel road after the last corner. She willed their car to come into view and wanted to be the first to fling open the gate and welcome them home.

The noise grew louder but it seemed to move slowly and didn't sound right, muffled by the tall sugar cane and straining, and at the last moment a rattling old blue bakkie came into view, piled high with firewood and laden down. It braked, then slowly turned away from her and disappeared from view. The old driver, grey bearded, with feathers lodged in his hair, waved but continued on his own way, leaving a trail of dust hanging in the air, nothing to do with her. As the dust settled, the sound of it passing into the afternoon sunlight died slowly away into a deathly quiet filled only with emptiness.

The owl had flown silently away at dusk sometime during the previous evening. She knew it had gone when the birds grew silent again. But something in the hidden mechanism of her life and world had been jarred and shaken in some way, and she sensed the change. That evening she'd prayed fervently and aloud for the safe return of her family, most especially Jackie and the little one whom she loved so dearly. Her voice rose and fell with the tide of her emotions, steeped in the richness of her own language as she thought about the owl, the children, her life.

All evening she waited, thinking that maybe they were stuck at the border or had a breakdown. Finally, and sadly, having fallen asleep several times, she put the dogs out, turned off the oven to save the supper, and went to bed. Another day of quiet had passed but instead of ending in happiness, the sun finally set on silence and loneliness. She wasn't sure how to phone overseas, but they had left some numbers. Perhaps tomorrow she would phone someone to ask for help. With that thought in her head faintly comforting to her she finally slept.

Saturday dawned uneasy and unsettled; the sky was grey, windy and overcast with high clouds racing across it as if all heading somewhere. She knew there were relatives in Johannesburg, and called them up during the morning. 'BabeMkhulu,' she said, 'do you know where are the Bartons? They were supposed to come yesterday, but they never came.'

The old father of Melanie sounded unsure. He said he didn't know but would try to find out. He called back about an hour later, saying the aeroplane left England late but he thought it must still be coming. That afternoon someone else rang, one of their friends, wanting to welcome the Barton family back. She explained, 'No, it's me Khanyi. They are not here; they are still coming.'

That evening the phone rang and this time it was the old father again, but now he sounded somehow different, unsure of himself, as if he wasn't telling her everything he knew.

'Khanyisile', he said, 'Khanyisile, listen my girlie, they think something has gone wrong with the aeroplane. They are not sure where they are. I will tell you what's happening when we find out more. Do you need money? Must I send you some money?'

She had met him several times before and now he sounded old and confused, not like his normal self. They made an arrangement to send some money to a farmer nearby that she knew well. He would bring her the money.

That night she tried to watch TV but couldn't settle. She watched a little of the news but switched it off and listened to the radio. When the 9.00pm news came on, the news reader uSimelane mentioned something about an aeroplane somewhere that was flying but it may have got lost in a storm. It was not certain what had happened. It was travelling from Europe to Africa. But she knew her family had already landed in South Africa and must be on their way. The date with the red ring around was now two days past. Probably one of the children was sick and they had to see a doctor in Jo'burg. That must be the reason why they were coming late. She didn't know who to ask for news.

Chapter 4

On the evening of the 17th of August the phone rang again and she could hear it was an overseas call. The voice sounded almost like her boss, but it was different and a bit younger. 'Khanyisile.' he said, 'this is Matt, Matt Barton, Mr. Barton's brother speaking. Khanyisile, I have to tell you some very sad news, is there someone you can be with today?'

She answered no, that she was alone in the house, only her and the dogs.

There was a gap and she wondered if the phone had gone off. Then he sighed.

'Khanyi,' he said, sounding as if he was starting to cry himself, 'Khanyi, I have to tell you that the Bartons are not going to come home.'

'Why!' she exclaimed 'Why? Is there any problem with the children? Are they sick? Did they come late? Did they have a breakdown on the plane? When are they going to come? Must I make fresh food for them?' She wanted to ask many questions.

'No, Khanyi, my dear. I am so sorry to tell you this over the phone. I wish you had someone to be with you. They are not ever going to come home. On the way some terrible people put a bomb inside the aircraft, and when it was over the ocean it exploded. Everyone inside is lost. They don't even know if we will ever find the place where they fell'.

She heard his voice change as he began crying himself as he told her. She had never met him, but had been shown pictures of him, the children's uncle Matthew. He looked a little bit like her little one and he was a lot like the boss, but a bit younger. They used to call him Matt.

She felt the same cold she had felt when she saw the owl. This was why it visited her. She could not speak. Her mind raced from one place to another, panicking like a wild bird caught in a thorn bush.

What about the little one's clothes, what about Jackie's school, what about Melanie and Mr. Barton? Where were they now? How could she find them to see them for the last time? What about their ancestors? What about the funeral? What can they have to bury? What about the dogs? the last bag of food was almost close to finish!

Her thoughts flew around randomly, alighting on everything and everywhere other than herself, then finally began to land and settle as she realised that her whole life, her work, her job, her family, her place to stay had all ended in this phone call. The phone was shaking in her hands.

Was this agony in her heart still punishment for her mistake at school? She could not speak. She felt faint and sick and cold all at once and let out a wail of absolute despair. Her stomach knotted. Matt was trying to hold himself together and comfort her from thousands of miles away, but he could only make the noises you make to soothe a baby. She barely heard him in her pain and time passed slowly, like when children are avoiding their chores and dragging their feet.

Her mind ran wildly into her childhood in the shock of the moment, flashing through her life.

'Yay wena!'

She remembered those words.

'Yay wena! Phakamisa tinyawo!'

Her grandmother would often shout at the children like that: 'Hey you, lift up your feet.'

'Be quick – get on with it!'

She loved the old lady, even though she was harsh and sometimes beat them. She was always taking snuff which seemed to make her energetic and issue even more than the usual instructions. She would send them on countless errands – go and make tea, go and bring water, go and carry firewood, go and look for eggs, go and bring a cabbage, go and find your mother.

When she felt tired of work, tired of ironing or polishing, she would hear that voice again and carry on. Her preacher had told them that life would improve one day if she worked hard enough. He had told them, "Lift up your feet and your heart will follow".

The day she gave birth was her worst memory. 'You are a stupid!' the nurses shouted, slapping her when she cried. 'You see now, eh heh! This is what happens when you are a rubbish. You like sleeping with your boyfriends too much! you are going to scream, now now, you are going to scream like a hell.'

When the pain began, she gasped and cried, but still heard through the veil of pain and fear the vastly fat matron with the shiny face panting and berating her, shouting above her cries, 'It's your fault, wenaKhanyisile, because you are skeberesh.' A prostitute! Was she really a prostitute because of one thing that happened?

The pain when it came was beyond her imagining and no one explained to her how long it would last or what was happening. She wanted to die. It was worse than a beating from her father, worse than the time when the female elders would take a mealie cob and scrape it against her lishashati, removing the poison from her infected tonsils, an illness she often suffered from as a child. That was the rural method, the harsh home cure. The mealie cob was used as a rasp to scrape off the infected areas and open up new flesh. It was a terrible pain.

The Bogogo, the village grandmothers, would hold her down and force her mouth open, and do the deed. The taste of blood and pus made her vomit and this was met with a chorus of approval from the wizened old crones, reeking of woodsmoke, pushing each other for a better view and all giving advice. 'Yebo!' they would shout at her loudly, 'it's good, it must come out, we have helped you to cleanse the evil from your body,' and then they would give her salt water to drink to make her vomit. For weeks afterwards she could not speak for the soreness of her throat.

She sensed deep within her what that owl signified, remembering how the elders and her preacher had told her so many times that her problem was she was full of black sin. The Umfundisi even said she was steeped in sin, but she never knew what steeped meant or if it could be undone. It sounded bad. He told her she was unclean. She had given birth to an unwanted daughter and her penalty was going to be a life of shame and sorrow. Ntombi (Mafikizolo) had only lived to the age of three, a neglected, trusting little toddler unable to be with her mother. She had not been well cared for by the step-mother and fell ill early in her third year, dying from dehydration, a combination of dirty water, lack of care, too little food and powdered milk. They had taken two days before even telling Khanyisile what had happened.

After her return from the government hospital with the baby, she could not even say the child's name for many months, remembering the sorrow of leaving school, a place that she had really loved. Khanyi hadn't even known that she really had a boyfriend. They had walked together a few times and he had spoken to her on the way home, once giving her sweets.

One evening coming from school together he pulled her into some long grass, then he covered her mouth and she felt her panties pulled down and a sharp pain inside. He told her that this showed how much he loved her even above the other girls. The act was over so quickly she had understood little of what was happening. He gave her five Rand and told her to keep quiet. When the girl was born he left school and was never seen again.

As any Swazi knew, an owl was always the harbinger of death. Whenever dreadful events had disrupted her life, an owl signifying death had always visited the homestead before the event. Remembering the phone call, she was suddenly reminded of all the worst moments in her short life.

She came back from her panicked thoughts to the empty house, the phone in her hand, and the voice on the other end.

'Khanyi, can you hear me, are you alright? Are you still there?'

They both spoke at once: She began, 'I am dead Mr. Matt, my heart is dead, all my life is finished.'

He started: 'Listen, I am coming out to help you, Khanyi. I am coming from England to help you. You won't be alone for long. My brother left instructions that I must sort everything out. I'm just trying to get on a flight, but it won't be long'. She only heard part of this...

'You are coming here, Mr. Matt? Coming here to this house from that side?'

'Yes,' he replied clearly, 'I am going to come there soon. In just a few more days, or maybe a week. I know where the house is, Khanyi. I've even seen it on the computer. My brother showed me.'

She had nothing to say to this. Everything had just become too much to take in. Overwhelmed and unable to speak any more she suddenly felt faint and whispered, 'Ngiyabonga, Mr. Matt,' forgetting to say it in English for him, and slowly put the phone down.

She slid down the wall onto the floor, covered her face in her hands, burst into tears and began sobbing. In her mother tongue she began pleading to God, berating Him. 'NkuluNkuluwami, why did you make this to happen, why have you taken them from me, why have you taken the little one and Jackie? They were my loved ones; they were my home.'

Sobbing as if her heart would break, her chest heaved and tears rolled down her cheeks and dripped onto the floor. Immediately, interested in the novel, unfamiliar sound, all the dogs gathered around her and began licking her wet face, puzzled but happy to have her at their level.

The more she wept the more they licked, snuffling and pressing their wet cold noses and muzzles into her face and leaning the weight of their warm bodies against her, almost as if they wanted her

to know they would always be there for her. The biggest ones leant against her shoulders.

They knew this was something unusual, having a big person to wash at floor level and took advantage of the opportunity. Each of them jostled for the prime position, trying to lick her straight in her face and lick away the salt tears. After a while, her tears began to subside and she stood up, as much to get away from the animals' cold noses and wet tongues as anything else.

She still felt sick but her mind eased a little as she slipped into a comforting and well worn routine.

She must feed the dogs, turn on the security lights, lock the gate. She washed her face and completed the chores automatically, hardly noticing where she was or what she was doing. Her life as she knew it had ended with that phone call. Soon she would be without a job and without money, with nowhere to live and no one to care for her. The pain she felt, thinking of losing those two children who were like her own, was unbearable.. She felt sick.

She put the dogs out, locked the doors and lay down, awake and unable to sleep, watching the bright moonlight bathing the garden in silver light and shadows. The tree where the owl had been perched was dead still. It grew quiet.

Chapter 5

On a normal week day, ten thousand kilometres to the North, Matt Barton had asked for an urgent meeting with Mr. Pearson, the Managing Director of the specialist service company he worked for. The rain teemed down outside, veiling much of a typically wet Lancashire landscape. The roads and fields were covered in sheets of water, most of the country shrouded by low grey clouds. His request had been agreed to and within days he was booked on a direct night flight, London to Johannesburg, with an onward connection to Swaziland. He had stood around for some time, then eventually sat down, waiting outside the big office on the third floor, pretending to read the trade publications but looking at his boss's very pretty young PA, Emma, out of the corner of his eye. She knew he was looking at her but didn't really mind. Most men usually did, and many people in the small engineering company knew and liked Matt. There was rather more going on behind the scenes than he ever knew about.

Matt was regarded as someone a bit special, someone likely to rise fast in the company. He was still quite young, unencumbered by family and able to travel at short notice. Matt was the best internationally certified and fully accredited double coded welder in the company, and one of only a handful in the whole country with his particular mix of skills. He had assembled a bewildering list of letters and numbers after his name, with many different qualification codes covering specialist welding techniques for a variety of particularly difficult materials. He'd initially trained in Britain, but then had been selected for more specialized training in the US, Germany and Japan, and he would be flown at a few days' notice to almost anywhere in the world to carry out the kind of impossibly difficult repairs in very awkward positions that only a handful of people knew how to do. For this expertise he was very highly valued in the organisation, and highly regarded.

In his short but busy career, he had been called to oil rigs in Bahrain and in the Gulf of Mexico, welded up gas pipelines in the Ukraine and Mozambique, and repaired oil pipelines and desalination plants in Nigeria and Saudi Arabia. He had worked with aircraft manufacturers in Europe and Russia, and had occasionally been called on to work inside warships, or on huge drag line excavators and tunnelling equipment. Once, he had even done emergency repairs to the leaking hull of a decompression chamber on a research vessel, somewhere in the North Atlantic, flown out to it by helicopter.

Matt had been to some very remote parts of the world, and spent most of his life inspecting huge complicated pieces of equipment that would sometimes have been scrapped, unless someone could successfully repair them, as they were too big or remote to move from wherever they were situated to somewhere that could mend them. He often only saw one small part of some sprawling chemical plant or a giant machine, the particular component or section that needed repairs, and he would sometimes fly back home wondering what the rest of it was for. It was an odd life, living like a dragonfly and seldom settling in one place for long, but he had enjoyed the steady stream of new sights and sounds, and the odd feeling he had, which he knew only a few people understood: that of being a global traveller, part of the world, not just a country.

Flying was such a frequent occurrence in his working life that there was little novelty left in it. In the past few days, after that terrible matter-of-fact unemotional phone call from the airline's legal representatives, he'd had to make several very important phone calls, courier various certified documents to insurance companies and family lawyers, received ghastly, emotionless, formally worded documents from the airline, have a deeply painful conversation with his sister-in-law's elderly parents, pack for a short trip, book a hire car, advise Khanyisile in Swaziland of his plans and remember all the other multitude of things required before making the journey.

Chapter 6

HE'D NEVER KNOWN WHAT HIS time was charged out at, nor did he really care, but he did vaguely know that he was among the highest paid welding technicians in the company, and that he usually earned far more than he spent. He neither knew nor cared what amount of money he currently had in the bank, but occasionally would get a call from some snooty bank type person who usually talked down to him, suggesting he moved money into an account that would earn interest, and he would often be surprised at the amount mentioned. He had a few investments that he largely ignored and seldom touched.

He loved welding. He loved the challenge of melding different materials together and completing difficult welds on special steels and alloys, and knowing exactly what special materials to order, which gases, welding supplies and obscure equipment he needed for each new repair job. He loved the molten pool of metal that he could move along with such skill, and such a steady hand. He sometimes felt as though he could perceive deep underneath the skin of the molten pool, sensing the dissimilar molecules losing their individual identity and joining to other new ones, to melt together and become stronger than they had even been on their own. He could feel the complex metallurgical theory coming to life before him, just as it was supposed to.

He liked to leave a finished welded seam that looked as if it had been created in a factory under perfect conditions. He was immensely proud of his workmanship, although he seldom admitted it, and took many things personally, especially any criticism of his workmanship.

He was a highly skilled specialist. He would often be flown over the last leg of journeys to the work sites by helicopter, and would have to calculate what materials were required, then carefully work out the welding angles and positions, sometimes visualising the repair over a few days, before making several incredibly costly satellite phone calls for twenty or thirty minutes at a time to Salikh, the Pakistani storeman back in Lancashire, a friend who knew him well and who understood the strange, deeply technical language that he spoke.

He'd order lists of special welding equipment, sometimes needing exotic gases and rare materials, and these would be air freighted out to him at great cost, finding him wherever he was.

While he waited he would spend a few days resting on a hotel bed, trying to follow foreign films on local TV or strolling around a strange town if there was one nearby, tasting new foods and trying to talk to the engineers and technicians on site until the equipment came.

He was used to being alone. His expense claims were minimal as he seldom drank much, and he generally kept to himself. His employers rarely queried anything he asked for because he either used it all or would send any leftovers back. Sometimes, during a long job in a particularly remote place, he would ask Salikh for a local paper, and this would come as packaging in the air freighted hardware. Then he would sit in his lonely hotel room in some remote part of the world and read articles about a flower show, a vandalised bus stop or a prize awarded for Best Rabbit at a local village fair and these odd, meaningless but comforting pieces of news somehow refreshed him and made him feel connected and strangely content. He knew there were people backing him at home.

Once he had everything ordered and planned for the work ahead, he would prepare himself rather like a professional hit man, rehearsing all the hand movements and changes of body position, steadily pulling the gas hoses and heavy cables through the surrounding framework to ensure there were no snarl ups. There were certain repair sections that had to be completed in one unbroken move.

He would practise the verticals, the overhead and difficult inverted runs, where and how he would start each run, how he would need to lie to squeeze his body into the available space, and work out the timing and when to move. All the snags and the stoppages to replace wire reels or gas, practising the process again and again in situ, until he felt ready to start and work with the longest possible unbroken runs. He was painstakingly thorough and very good at what he did.

With everything to hand, he would put on his protective clothing and gloves – always in the same order, and always wearing the same filthy old black welding cap – then flip down his visor and start working. He would usually work right through those long days, completing hours and hours of intensely difficult, mentally focused, highly technical welding and machining without a break, until the repair was completed.

He would ask only for tea, soft drinks and sandwiches, always of the same type, and stop only to rest his eyes, to ease some tired muscles, to eat, or to let the equipment cool down. He was used to working very intensively on these trips and would often be tired for a few days afterwards as his body recovered.

The invoices, when they arrived after his departure, would usually run into tens of thousands of dollars for a few days' work, a consideration the clients were happy to pay, as well as his flights and accommodation, because that cost was invariably far less than the millions of dollars they were losing by holding up production. He fixed things, but he fixed very big things that other people couldn't fix or didn't know how to.

Chapter 7

AFTER A FEW MINUTES WAITING outside with Emma, the boss had called him in, and Matt began to explain the situation to him. The news of the loss of his elder brother and family had spread through the business like a virus. The older man of the two actually knew rather more than he was letting on, because he was a good MD who cared for his staff and had people who discretely told him these things, so he let Matt sit down, gather his thoughts and say his piece. He liked him.

After briefly explaining the events of the past few days, and what was known about the loss of the aircraft, Matt finished by saying quietly, 'So, Mr. Pearson, what it is, is that I need to ask for some personal time off, to go and sort out my brother's affairs, wrap up the property, deal with things over there and then I'll be back in a few weeks or so, but I can't say exactly when until I get there.'

Brian Pearson, MD, drawing on a wealth of experience, first expressed how sorry he was to hear the sad news, asking Matt to pass on his condolences, then, making an immediate decision, said, 'Of course you must go Matt, we quite understand. You have a lot of leave owing. Take what you need and if there's anything we can do from our side, let me know personally and I'll try to help. If we can help to book flights or sort out any other details, let Emma know, and she'll take care of it.'

He meant it. And he felt rather foolish afterwards, for passing on condolences to a lad with no other family.

There were few staff members as valuable to him as this loyal, rather intense, hardworking young man who often brought into the firm over a million pounds of work each year. He hoped the process of wrapping up the estate would be completed quickly, knowing that they were coming into the latter part of the year when they tended to became extremely busy. As a metallurgist himself, and something of a specialist in his own right, Brian Pearson knew what skills he had in Matt and how hard it would be to replace him.

Matt, equally, knew that Pearson genuinely cared for his staff. There were many stories, corporate legends often retold in the workshops and back offices of the firm, about families that had unexpectedly received some financial help during a rough patch, or of young couples getting a voucher for a free dinner after one of them had been away for several weeks for work, or staff going through a rough time being offered a free weekend away, all courtesy of Brian Pearson. He had an uncanny skill at seeming to know who was facing domestic trouble in his business. He would ignore advice, and often disregard much of what his HR advisors told him, much to their annoyance, and he simply ignored protocols, doing whatever he felt was right.

He was known to keep his ears very close to the ground indeed, and would often surprise someone totally, like when he asked the Spanish night shift cleaning lady about how her husband's back operation had worked out, or enquired from the receptionist at the front desk if their eldest son had managed to get his county colours for cricket.

The lovely Emma was said to be a key part of his slick intelligence gathering operation, but she ran this so subtly and tactfully that no one really knew how he knew what he knew, but although he was always discrete about it, it was often said in the corridors and workshop floors that there was one thing for sure: our Mr. Brian bloody Pearson knew bloody nearly everything that went on. He also ran a very profitable business.

They shook hands after their meeting, and Matt thanked him and walked out, having been authorized to take compassionate leave almost immediately. Emma said goodbye and watched him turn and walk away, thinking how tired and pale he looked. The tragic news that they had by now all heard about had somehow aged him.

Chapter 8

IT HAD BEEN STRESSFUL, EMOTIONALLY wearing and deeply tiring. He began to feel drowsy even while the plane was still taxiing away from the airport buildings, and sat back as the familiar chant about safety belts, upright seats and electronic devices washed over him and he let his mind wander, drifting over the awful events of the last few days. It had been a terrible shock to realise he had lost his elder brother, but to lose the whole family in one dreadful event, just weeks after spending so many special, laughter-filled days with them during their European holiday, was still very hard to take in. It was almost too painful to remember. He remembered saying goodbye to them at Heathrow after their short holiday, and hugging his niece and nephew tightly after getting to know each of them a little better. It had been an amazing few weeks, a time that had somehow brought them all closer together.

They were his closest family. He was very fond of his sister-in-law and, albeit as a distant uncle, he doted on both the children, having none of his own. He loved talking to them and the way their inquisitive young minds worked.

The big jet turned slowly and braked to a halt, rocking gently and positioning itself at the farthest end of the rain-soaked runway. As the pilots ran up the four huge engines, they raised long rooster tails of spray, lifting sheets of water off the runway and creating great vapour trails behind each jet. Ripples like a speedboat's wake spread out behind them on the tarmac. After a short pause, they were cleared for takeoff, and the aircraft began to accelerate, pushing each passenger deep into their seats as the thrust increased.

He watched the rain drops trickling slowly down over the cabin window, distorting the dreary grey view outside, and then beginning to streak sideways across the window as the aircraft's speed increased, and he closed his eyes, wondering dully about what he might have forgotten. He was very tired.

As the heavy aircraft reached its take off speed, it gently eased free from the bonds holding it onto the earth and became a thing of the air, and he dreamily gazed out at the wet city lights. Thousands of headlights reflecting off the dark soaking tarmac in long snaking lines. He pushed his seat back a little and quickly fell asleep, emotionally shattered, numb and physically exhausted.

Bleary eyed the next morning, in need of a wash and a shave and a little disorientated, he arrived, along with hundreds of other passengers and patiently made his way along the mind-deadening serpentine queue through to immigration. He passed through, eventually retrieved his battered, well-travelled luggage and then found his way to the check in counters for the next flight and went through into the next departure lounge. He had time for a coffee, and then, feeling quite wide awake now, he left South African soil and boarded another, much smaller plane for the next leg of his journey.

It was over almost before it had begun, after barely forty-five minutes flying time, when they began to descend over the Swazi bushveld into the quiet afternoon. He watched as the stunted, flat topped trees, thorny scrub, cattle trails and sugar cane fields first emerged as a grey blue haziness and then came into sharp focus, turning into lifelike miniature scenery beneath him as they came in to land. Towards the end of winter the land below looked dry and dusty, with patches of tawny, pale yellow grassland.

He was treated with exquisite politeness, charming smiles and respect at the airport, and was soon shown to his spotlessly clean hire car, and then given friendly instructions how to get onto the right road. It was late afternoon and shadows were lengthening, the bare trees casting their presence in patches across the broad road verges. The previous long hours of travelling were beginning to make themselves felt, and he drove carefully, conscious of his weariness and of the frequent roaming cattle and occasional unexpected goats that wandered into the road. The afternoon light was somehow sharp and very different, and it felt a long way from rainy Lancashire. Matt became acutely aware of the feeling that his brother Patrick would have driven along this road hundreds of times and had seen everything that he was seeing, but with much more accustomed eyes.

As though he was driving on a well-worn path home, the spiritual remnants of his family remained on it like traces left behind from previous sunlit days. He drove along and sensed a deep solitude, and the weight of his responsibility, and without thinking began to speak out loud, talking to his elder brother again, using their childhood names. "God help me through this, Pat. I've never done anything like this before, and I don't want to mess it up. I really want to do this properly for you, brother. I just can't believe what's happened."

After driving for some time he saw the small numbered signboard marking the little district road that led to the house. He turned off and drove along a narrow, rough, potholed dirt road, with long stands of tall sugar cane lining each side of the route.

Every so often he would hear tall overhead sprinklers making an odd tsk.. tsk.. tsk.. tstststs sound he had never heard before, as they made their way around and over the road, splashing a muddy arc across the surface, momentarily splattering the passenger windows with loud heavy drops, wetting sections of the windscreen and washing clean streaks in the dust on the side of the car. He began to feel uneasy and unsure of himself. He didn't know it, but the sugar cane was in flower at that time of year, and the late afternoon sun shone through the wispy white inflorescence reaching high and slender above the tall cane stalks. The world seemed to close in on him, and his surroundings became even more concentrated, engulfing him in endless, rolling hectares of green sugar cane with a distinctive smell, growing tall and impenetrable, lush and even, as far as the eye could see.

He occasionally heard a faint rustling of something unseen as the evening air moved through the leaves of the tall stands of vividly green canc. The deserted, bumpy, gravel road beckoned him on into the distance and a muted homecoming awaited him. The light was fading fast now and he turned on the car's headlights. It seemed odd having no street lights.

Deep within himself he felt both unprepared and inadequate, and silently hoped for the right words to say to Khanyisile. He had been so busy thinking of everything else that he had not given enough thought to how to handle this first meeting, and he was acutely aware of his lack of preparation. It hadn't occurred to him to ask anyone – how could you prepare for this?

His Swaziland family had mentioned many times how much they valued her and the important role she played in their busy household. The occasional phone conversations with her while on holiday clearly meant a lot to them, and they always came back from the phone excited, talking animatedly about home. She had been a very important part of their lives here, but he had no idea how their relationship had really worked.

He was the newcomer now but, instead of facing the familiar scene of a complex piece of broken steel and another industrial site, he was going to have to deal with a shattered relationship, and he had no training to rely upon to guide him forward. Nothing he could order from Salikh would help. He drove over a small canal and then, remembering the satellite pictures, he turned off again onto a narrow farm track with long grass and dense paper thorns growing along the verges, continuing until he saw an unmarked farm gate in the gathering dusk. Someone was moving slowly towards the gatepost and had begun loosening a chain. The person opened the gate for him and he turned in, waving thanks at a rough male figure in a khaki shirt who looked like a gardener of some kind. He must have been waiting patiently in the gathering dusk for his arrival. He thought again of how little he really knew of his brother's lifestyle out here.

A large, sprawling, well kept bungalow loomed into view, set among big spreading lawns under old flamboyant and big hardwood trees, some of them bare of leaves, and he slowly drove up the tidy drive towards the house, the car tyres crunching on gravel. A large, mixed pack of dogs immediately got up and trotted towards the car, some growling with hackles raised, others sniffing the air and wagging their tails, seemingly knowing, as dogs do, that this was an expected guest and not an intruder. They went straight up to each tyre and smelt it deeply.

He got out of the car as she came out of the house, and his first impressions were how thin she looked and how formally she was dressed. He felt a bit unkempt and scruffy in comparison.

She walked lightly towards him and took his hand with both of hers, holding him in a surprisingly strong grip. 'Welcome, Mr. Matt, you have come. Thank you, thank you for coming, Mr. Matt.' She looked down as she spoke. He mumbled something in return about being pleased to meet her, but the right words got in the way of each other and failed him. Khanyi felt a sudden wave of relief wash over her. Having someone arrive to help at last meant so much, and her eyes filled with tears. She gasped and let out a sob. He freed his hand and simply hugged her to him tightly; it instinctively seemed the right thing to do.

He felt her chest begin to move as she took deep sobbing breaths and began to cry with relief, and he was suddenly overwhelmed by everything too, greatly affected by her emotions. For the second time since hearing the news his eyes filled with tears, thinking about their lost family and what they had meant to them both.

They stood closely together in the darkening driveway, wiping away tears and talking and sniffing and both trying in vain to keep up some appearances – she as the housekeeper and most trusted family servant, he as the visiting brother and sole heir, finally coming out from the UK to attend to wrapping up the family's affairs after too many days had passed.

In the end, he need not have worried about the actual words he said. There are times when there is nothing anyone can say without sounding awkward, or striking a wrong note. He followed his instincts, and said little, letting his humanity and actions speak for him. Khanyisile felt at last that she could release some of the tension she had been holding in for so long, and could finally talk to someone again, a somebody who had grown up with her boss, and knew the family well, but she was still a little nervous about meeting him. She didn't know Matt apart from seeing some pictures of him.

Matt was an uncomplicated man without false pretences. He knew why he had come, he knew what he had to do, and he was not a person to try and be something he was not. He had never really encountered a house servant in his life and found it difficult to relate or position himself in this new world he had come to. He had very few preconceived notions. Khanyisile, the big house here, his role and the new country were like an unopened book to him. He was conscious of his own naiveté and wanting to do the right thing. None of his technical training or experience could help him here. He felt that he was on his own.

Having been a blue collar worker all of his life, albeit a highly skilled one, he often thought back to the times he had been made to feel uncomfortable by others more senior to him, and he always tried to avoid coming across in a similarly dismissive or condescending way to any people he met. It was an approach that helped him make friends and headway easily in many countries.

Matt's education and most of his work had been in environments in which race was largely immaterial or went unnoticed. He knew that different cultures had very different beliefs and conventions, but he carried no other baggage. People were people.

'I'm so sorry Khanyisile,' he said, over and over again. 'I can't tell you how sorry I am.'

After a little time they drew apart but still held onto each other's hands, drawing strength from one another. They both took in the new person they were seeing under the outside lights, as it had grown almost dark.

Just as she began to say, 'Hau, Mr. Matt, you must be too tired, you have come a long way,' drawing out the word *long* as if to illustrate the distance itself, he also spoke and asked, 'What about you? Are you alright, Khanyi? How are you doing, are things alright here?'

'I am still okay, and the house is all okay. I made something to eat. Do you want food? I tried to make something, but I am not so good in cooking.'

Matt was suddenly aware that the last time he had eaten was during the long flight, almost a day ago, after being woken at some ungodly hour for breakfast by an unreasonably vivacious, groomed and charming young flight attendant, in the pre dawn a full two hours before landing, and he felt that he could certainly eat now.

'Food would be great, Khanyisile. That would be really great, thanks.'

They went in, she insisting on carrying some of his luggage, which didn't amount to much.

He didn't really know the niceties about who to address as Sis', and who not to, but he had often heard the children and his sister talk about SisKhanyi, and thought it might set her at ease even if he pronounced it wrong. He found himself very much wanting to avoid coming across as her boss.

They walked in together, she respectfully refusing to go ahead of him through the front door, and he was shown an immaculate spare room where he would be staying. Several dogs followed them in, eager to be part of this new development and monitoring proceedings closely. He wasn't their proper family, they sensed this, yet he seemed to be somehow similar to the alpha male they knew from before. He almost smelt like their old family and didn't appear to be any threat, either to their human Khanyisile, who had been feeding them, or to the home. They followed and watched him closely.

Darkness fell and shrouded the home, peaceful and silent, lying restfully in its nightdress of trees and gardens, set deep among the cane fields, gently lit by the grace of the moon. As the dogs roamed around before digging their sleeping pits, curling up and settling, security lights would switch on and off, lighting up areas of smooth lawn and neat flower beds.

Chapter 9

KHANYI SWITCHED ON THE HOUSE lights and began to heat up some food, while he laid his suitcase on the bed and took out a few of his things. He began to walk around the house, noticing some familiar objects: books he had grown up reading as a child, pictures of their parents, pictures of him on the beach during a long ago Greek holiday, smiling into the camera and looking much younger.

Pictures of his brother on their sunny wedding day, looking a bit thinner, proudly standing with his arms wrapped tightly around his young bride's slim waist. Formal pictures of the two children, both as babies. A picture of Jackie asleep in a car seat, still clutching tightly onto a teddy bear.

A perfectly timed and oddly intimate photograph of Melanie wearing a swimming costume, looking back over her shoulder at the camera as if caught by surprise, her tanned legs dangling over a waterfall. It took pride of place on the sideboard. She had been a lovely person and he had always admired her. He felt a strange mixture of feelings, on one hand familiar and almost at home, but at the same time like a voyeur seeing private parts of a life from which he had always lived apart. It was a strange sensation and he was grateful when Khanyi came to the doorway of the room, knocking softly and breaking his revelry.

'The food is ready, Mr. Matt.'

'Call me Matt, Khanyi, just call me Matt,' he asked.

She thanked him, but still said, 'Yes Mr. Matt, I will do it like that.'

He was too tired to ask again.

Matt took people at face value – whether he was trying to understand the grumbling complaints of a Ukrainian tea lady about the shortage of sugar, or attending an Initial Scope Assessment meeting with the Iranian Engineering Director of an Oil Multinational.

He saw all people in the same way and seldom promoted himself, or pushed himself to the forefront. He relied on his skills to provide him with credence and carry him through first encounters. In some ways he lacked self-assurance, and he had very little personal vanity. With no deeply ingrained attitudes about race, people's skin colour was as immaterial to him as their hair colour, and of little meaning. He had grown up and worked in a multinational environment where the Indian man wearing blue overalls, safety boots and a high visibility safety vest might be the tea maker, or might be the Engineering Director, so his mind was open.

He saw Khanyi firstly as good company, and not as a domestic worker. People themselves mattered to him more than what they did. Unpleasant people didn't really bother him much. He had often encountered rude and aggressive men on different work sites, especially in Russia, Holland and Croatia, but they didn't affect him for long. He was seldom in one place long enough for them to trouble him deeply and he usually had a specific job to complete. Mostly the relationships outside of his work were fleeting and short lived.

There had been a sort of on-off girlfriend he had been seeing for a while, Jess, one of those utterly cynical, down to earth British girls who would take the piss if ever he tried to be romantic or act sentimental, and would often tease him about it afterwards when he did. They had slept together a few times, and she had told her mates in the pub what it was like, which had upset him. She invariably wore black jeans and heavy boots, and usually dyed her hair jet black as well. Her expectations were low, based on her experience of men, and she wasn't about to change them just for one exception even though she was vaguely fond of Matt. When he went to explain to her about leaving, she said she was sorry about his loss and all, but they both knew she wasn't really bothered one way or the other about him going and, if he were honest, neither was he. She had then told him about her new tattoo and insisted he look at it.

They'd parted on friendly terms, she said her usual, 'Tara then, luv,' and gave him a peck on the cheek, and a close hug (a rarity from her) but they both knew that it was probably a convenient ending for whatever it was they had shared. She was fun when she was in a good mood, but could also be very blunt and cutting, especially after a few drinks, and he hadn't ever particularly wanted her to meet his family or any of his closer friends.

A table had been laid for one, and he asked Khanyi if she would join him, but she had eaten earlier and respectfully placed hot food on the table, some rice and a simple chicken stew. She then made as if to retire to the kitchen but he called her back. 'Please come sit with me, Khanyi. I want to know what things you need here.'

She seemed a little uneasy about this but sat at the far end of the table and explained they did need some things for the house, especially food for the animals, and that there were some workers who needed paying. There was a list she had made. She offered to make him some tea. Matt agreed and chatted to her over his drink about these domestic issues. Then, beginning to tire, he suggested they would sort it all out in the morning. She agreed and left, saying she was going to sleep. He escorted her to the back door, a bit confused by this move.

She had a small garden cottage on the edge of the property, and for the first time since her family had left on holiday, she said goodnight to someone else in the home, preparing to leave and return to her own house to sleep. He noticed she even wished the dogs goodnight too. Recognising the sound of words they knew and knowing the time had come, they all reluctantly rose, stretching and turning around, and gradually trooped outside, following her. They were very protective over her, escorting her to the gate near her door.

Matt had never had pets to contend with before, and asked what he should do with them all. She told him that they all slept outside, and all had their own boxes to sleep in.

'Thank you for the dinner, Khanyisile. It was perfect.'

'Thank you Mr. Matt, for coming. It is good you are here now. I will see you tomorrow,' she replied.

He watched her slender figure walking across the garden towards her little house. It was all very different out here. She was quite young but seemed both subdued and very respectful, compared to someone of her age from the young people he knew back in Lancashire. He thought she looked quite pretty, with her hair combed straight back and tied tightly in a little tuft at the back of her head. It was hardly a pony tail. Her hair gleamed. She wore no makeup, as far as he could tell, and almost no jewellery. He was observant and had noticed many things about her, and watched her walking away under the moonlight, thinking idly that she seemed naturally graceful.

Khanyi walked across the narrow strip of land between the house and her home and thought to herself that he looked like a kind somebody, almost kind like his brother. He looked a bit like her boss, but he was a lot younger and looked more up to date. She had a keen eye for clothes, and noticed that he had a modern style of dressing she had not seen before, and hair that was very short. He had behaved very openly towards her. He even wanted to help carry plates and clear the table, which was awkward as it was her work. She hoped he found the house clean enough. He seemed to be nice towards her.

She opened up her cottage, prepared herself for bed and lay down to sleep, mostly worrying about how long it would be before her job ended and she would have to find a new family. Perhaps he could help her. He seemed to be a proper somebody.

In separate houses and each dreaming their separate dreams, the two young people drifted off to sleep.

Chapter 10

THINGS OFTEN LOOK BETTER IN the clean morning light, and Matt woke from a deep sleep, wondering for a moment where he was. The door seemed to be in the wrong place, and he tried opening a door to what he thought should be the bathroom but found it was a cupboard. He couldn't find his alarm clock and couldn't hear the normal morning traffic, the milk man or the buses rolling past his house. All he could hear were birds singing, and African voices shouting to each other, someone laughing at a funny story some distance away. He thought he could hear a tractor engine idling somewhere. It was unusually quiet in the room. He was disorientated for a second or two and then, in a rush of feelings, everything came back to him at once. This was his brother and Mel's home. This was their spare room. They were all gone now and this was what he had come for. It depressed him instantly.

After he was up and dressed, Khanyisile appeared and greeted him warmly, with a dazzling smile, fed the dogs and showed him around the kitchen and house, and where the study was. He hunted for cornflakes, his morning staple, opening cupboard after cupboard in vain, but made do with some coffee and toast.

'Let's make a list, Khanyi,' he said. 'You tell me what you need and then we can go and get the stuff.' She proffered the list, but he asked her to join him at the table. They tackled this little task jointly, and he felt a slight frisson along his spine as he listened to her carefully reciting and explaining each item, neatly written out, and watched her making a careful mark alongside each one. She knew exactly what each one cost, and if there was a cheaper option from another store.

Somehow he was fascinated by the way she pronounced the words and the care with which she spoke, as though she were measuring each word for value and using it sparingly. He had noticed that when she spoke in her own language to people outside she spoke far more rapidly, and was quicker in response.

'What about money, Khanyi? D'you not need some money now? You'll have to tell me what you need, so I can get that too.'

The double negative confused her. What did he mean do you not need something? Does he think I don't need money?

The confusion showed on her face and he rephrased what he meant without the double negative.

She was very bashful about this question, but eventually showed him a special book in which each month's pay was recorded; he thought it looked like Melanie's handwriting. It was complicated because there was also an additional amount for housesitting, and the housesitting had gone on for longer than they had planned, but they worked it out together. He was a bit shocked because he had thought it would be much more.

Then he began the process of opening the drawers in the filing cabinet, going through them carefully until he found what he was looking for. His brother had been an organised man and diligent in his financial affairs.

There were four deep drawers, each one partly full of cream cardboard folders, each divided by their simple labels; House and Family, Money and Finance, Cars and Garden and Galloway Consulting.

He started removing the hanging files, and opening up the folders until near the back of the Money and Finance drawer he found an envelope simply named Barton Will and Testament.

He already knew he was the executor of the estate. They had both exchanged documents and agreed to undertake this for each other some years ago, after Pat got married. In the event of my death… it began.

As he read through the formal phrases, pursuant to, and insofar as, these whereupons and successions led him to seek out various other folders and documents by name, and he began to realise that his elder brother, in the event that their entire family deceased, had left everything he owned to him, all the assets, and that this amounted to a very substantial sum both in cash holdings and assets.

There were several different life insurances, several savings accounts, investment funds and legacies, the house he was in, some land, a flat they leased out in Durban, equipment and all the vehicles. Patrick Seamus Barton had taken out a ninety-nine year lease on an established farmhouse, but sub-let the grazing land that went with it. It had a small workshop area at the rear, a little way from the homestead, and a large number of mostly antiquated tools, together with some more modern ones, a few work benches, gas welding bottles and other typical old farmyard debris scattered around. Pat made little use of this old equipment but it had come with the property.

Matt hadn't realised quite how well they had been doing for the last few years. The Barton's business, Galloway Consulting, had offered highly sought after and well paid professional services, advising on irrigation and agronomy to several commercial estates, a number of individual farmers, and a few large cooperative farms and estates, and his brother had been very successful in this, the income from it funding their lives. It extended well beyond sugar cane, as there was also correspondence between his brother and pecan nut growers, citrus farms, a few potato farmers and various other concerns. He was also doing some advisory work with the Ministry of Agriculture and their extension officers. He seldom spoke about his work because few people outside of agriculture found it interesting.

There was much correspondence and several technical reports that he did not understand, referring to various soil types, wetting periods, recommended gradients and layouts and other terminology that meant little to Matt. He realised he would have to write to each of the clients, advising them of what had happened, and in some cases refunding them for partial consultancies that would never be completed. This was going to be a lot more involved than he had imagined.

Khanyi knocked at the door and looked in, asking if he would like to have some tea. Matt was surprised to see how much time had passed; it was already late morning. He smiled at her and agreed and she came back with a tea tray, very English, with a knitted tea cosy and good china, but the whole ensemble set off by a teaspoon already stuck in the cup. He had assumed she would join him, but she had to be persuaded to do this, and she went to get another cup. She took her tea black. Matt was used to strong tea sloshed into a large mug, brewed up many times a day, and drunk in between jobs with filthy hands, and he struggled to hold the tiny handle on the delicate bone china tea cup.

Khanyisile watched him drinking, amazed that he didn't need sugar, and said, 'The AmaZion don't drink tea, Mr. Matt. They say Joko makes them dizzy, then they can easily become agents of Satan.'

'What's Joko, Khanyi, and who are the AmaZion?'

She laughed. 'It's a tea, Mr. Matt; it's a tea in a red box. But it's very strong so it makes you dizzy. The red gown Zionists say it makes you dizzy then demons will attack you and make you agents of Satan.'

He was learning fast. In all his travels he hadn't heard of demonic possession flowing directly from something as innocent as drinking tea, but he was glad she was making conversation, so he asked her with a smile, 'Sis Khanyi, which one do you like?'

She named a brand and he made a mental note to buy plenty of that one. She had coped with such a lot, and he wanted to make it up to her.

It seemed she didn't drink coffee at all, having been told not to by the church she attended. He wasn't much of a church goer, but didn't think that the Church of England warned against coffee.

More things to learn.

He made a long list of numbers to call, and started on the wearisome process of calling them, mostly in South Africa but some in Britain, phoning them one after another and advising them that his brother – and he had to give the full name, ID number, and all the painful details every time – had been killed in an air crash, and he was named in the will as the executor and inheritor and was visiting the house in order to begin the process of wrapping up the estate. Most of them asked for proof of various things, and needed certified copies, often original hard copies, and he made another list of which firm needed what documents, planning to spend the afternoon faxing, posting and emailing them. He found his way around the home computer quite easily but tying things up was becoming more complicated.

They needed supplies and fuel for the home and time was passing. He asked Khanyi to come with him, and they found the keys, started up one of the bakkies and left the house. She directed him, pointing out landmarks along the way. They drove to a small village nearby, where there was a basic supermarket, butchery, bottle store and a few other essential outlets including a post office, and he cleared out the Barton's tightly stuffed mailbox. They bought most things they needed from the list of items, and he included three boxes of cornflakes, all of them several months past their sell by date. With everything packed away, they drove back and between them put away their simple shopping.

As the afternoon wore on, he began the wearisome task of trying to fax documents to various offices and places in South Africa and the UK. The phone lines were erratic and the signal weak.

He had also seen that in the will there was a substantial amount directly payable to Khanyisile herself, which he hadn't discussed with her. He found out that she had a bank account of her own, and with his brother's bank details to hand, phoned the bank manager and made immediate arrangements for this amount to be paid over from a seven-day call account.

Then, after they had scratched together a simple late lunch, he asked her to come with him to the study and asked her, 'Khanyi, do you know my brother left many different instructions to be carried out after his death?'

'What must I do, Mr. Matt?' she replied. 'Please tell me so that I can do it.'

'No, Khanyi, its nothing like that. I mean Patrick left things for me to do or to check that they were done properly.'

'Oh, I see,' she said, looking a bit puzzled.

'You see, Khanyisile, they liked you very much and wanted to be sure you would be alright for a long time to come if anything bad happened to them.'

'Like an accident?' she asked.

'Yes, like that, or what has happened now to their plane.'

She looked puzzled, and asked if it was like a pension.

'Well, it's sort of something like that, but they left an instruction to me, that some money must be given to you, to thank you for all the years you have been with them.'

'Are you sure?' she said, thinking that this was unlikely. She had been their domestic worker.

'I am absolutely sure, Khanyi. It's written clearly in the will. Would you like to know what it is?'

'You can tell me, Mr. Matt.'

'Khanyisile, you will have to show me your ID, so I can write down that I've seen it, even though I know who you are. Then I will be transferring a hundred and forty-four thousand Emalangeni into your account, as soon as the bank releases it.'

Khanyi's eyes widened and she exclaimed, 'Hau! Are you sure, Mr. Matt? Is it right?'

He explained that his brother had recorded the date she started working for them, and a few years ago, when they'd updated their will, he had recorded that she must get R16 000 for each year or greater part of a year she was with them. This money had been set aside in a fund for her every year.

So now it came to this amount, and they had instructed that she should keep some of the money for when she became old, like a pension. She could have up to half in cash. He explained what that sum came to.

Khanyi's eyes filled with tears and she left the room. It was far more money than she had ever had, or even dreamt of having, and she was scared of such a sum. Matt let her collect herself, and after a little while she returned.

'Mr. Matt, can you help me with this money when it comes? I am scared that they may come to steal it.'

He was confused by this but realised she thought she would be given bags of cash.

'Of course I will,' he replied. 'I'll try and find out what you can do with that over here, and we will set something up for you, but it won't all be with you right now. You can leave it in the bank where it will be safe and you can take out how much you need.'

'I can be grateful. The people in town, those guys can easily cheat you, and then you are left with nothing.'

'Don't worry, Sis Khanyi, we will make sure it's safe,' he added, not knowing how, but certain that he would try. One of the financial companies in the files must be able to help him.

'But please, Khanyi, just call me Matt.'

'I'm going to try by all means, Mr. Matt,' she responded, smiling bashfully.

That evening, Khanyi had to attend church and Matt made himself a solitary dinner from the afternoon's shopping, and then sat outside watching the sun go down. Once the farm workers had finished, at about four, it suddenly became very peaceful. He went and sat on the porch.

The dogs gathered around him, gazing into the distance with their golden eyes and picking up on the sense of quiet. His mind wandered to the firm, to Brian Pearson, to Emma, and to the process he was going through. There was little chance of everything being completed in the fortnight he had planned. It was likely to take months, but that would mean leaving Khanyi alone for another long spell, and something made him reluctant to do that. She was a very open person, a young woman of similar age, and was a great help to him. He wondered idly what clothes she wore in her own time, and how she looked when she wasn't working.

Chapter 11

THE FOLLOWING DAY, HE WAS struggling with the frustrating process of trying to get faxes and messages through on an unreliable phone line when he heard a lawnmower starting up. It was running very badly, popping and misfiring, growing steadily worse and worse. Finally, the engine noise ceased entirely, and then he heard the noise of someone trying to restart it, muttering, tugging on the pull cord again and again. He was trying to feed the last page into a six page fax connection to Pretoria when Khanyi came to him, knocking gently at the door, and said that the gardener wanted to see him. He had met this elderly gent already, and found him very hard to follow. He spoke a very pure and regional form of SiSwati, with no English words included, and Khanyi would translate, but even she couldn't translate everything. She had explained that she also found it hard to understand all that he said, because he was speaking a deep version of the ancient language, not often used nowadays except in the rural areas. It was pure, the purest uncontaminated SiSwati from years gone by, and the elderly man relished his mastery of it.

The old chap was standing by the kitchen door with a fine red feather lodged upright in his greying hair, pushing before him an equally ancient lawnmower.

'Sawubona Mnumzane,' he said, greeting him traditionally with both his hands raised.

'Thismygrasscutmshin for Mr. Button ishavegotfuckedup.' It was the first time he had ever heard him speak in English.

Matt glanced at Khanyi, expecting her to be shocked, but she simply relayed to him 'Ndepethe he says that the grass cutting machine is completely buggered now and it no more works.'

He realised that there was an unspoken expectation that he would be able to mend this lawnmower, and asked her to tell Ndepethe to push it to the garage. He would look at it as soon as he had got the last page through the fax machine. The old man pushed it away, grumbling and muttering to himself, and Khanyi started smiling to herself, covering her mouth.

'What did he say, Khanyi?'

'Hmm! I can't say it, Mr. Matt…'

'No you must tell me – what was he saying?' Matt said, smiling.

'Hau! He's very rude that one. He says he doubt if you can fix it because you are still young and even Mr. Barton he also couldn't fix it before, and he's older than you.'

Matt chuckled. He had loved his brother dearly and knew he'd been a gifted academic and economist, but he was no mechanic. He thought he had a pretty good chance of getting it going again, probably much better than Pat. It took him all of twenty-five minutes to identify and repair the problem, opening up the points and cleaning the spark plug, and the elderly Briggs and Stratton burst into life in a cloud of white smoke, revving up and sounding far happier than it had for several years.

Coming hastily to the garage as soon as he heard the engine running, Ndephete very nearly smiled, his face reluctantly using muscles that had seldom been used before. Matt even thought he could see moisture in his dark eyes.

He thanked the young Mnumzane, grasping his hands firmly with his heavily calloused hands, and went off chortling to himself. In days to come, Matt would become aware that he loved that old lawn mower more than anything else in his world.

Khanyi was most impressed. She told him that Ndepethe was now very happy and soon would be asking for more petrol. She said that the Bartons had tried many times to buy a new one for him, but he always refused.

'He like that machine too much,' she said. 'He don't like it if anyone else uses it.'

She explained that he knew his machine was made by the Queen of England – it had a royal crest on the frame – but he believed that all new machines are no good because they are made by Amachayina – the Chinese – and are unreliable and weak in nature. Only the ones from the Queen were strong.

Over the next few days, in between dealing with the complicated paperwork and responding to some important registered mail that had begun arriving, Matt was shown a little about the local land by Khanyi. He learned where more small local shops were, visited the butchery and the nearest bank, drew out some money, and then was shown the clinic, a distant sugar mill, the road to a neighbouring farmer's house and several other places, including a small club, famous for its Thorn Tree restaurant.

Chapter 12

KHANYISILE SEEMED TO KNOW AN incredible number of people, and she'd often ask him to stop the car for her to greet them. This greeting was not a brief exercise. It usually involved a complex exchange of news. She would introduce him as the brother of the late Mr. Barton, and everyone he met seemed to know Patrick and would grip his hands and say, 'Hau! Shame, shame, sorry, sorry,' and express their deep sorrow at his loss. Some would express in very formal English their deepest condolences and sympathies to the family, mentioning how young Mr. Barton was, how much they liked his wife and even asking him to convey their respects and greetings to his father.

It didn't seem appropriate to tell them that his parents had both died years ago, so he just accepted these heartfelt and sincere expressions as best he could.

As an Englishman he wasn't used to such broad and public involvement in what was essentially his own personal grief, but began to realise that anyone who came into contact with Khanyi, or who knew her, and anyone she had helped, pretty much ever, was now linked in some remote way to her employers.

Their death was somehow everyone's death and a reason for grieving. He began to realise that unlike in Britain, where he would essentially bear the loss privately, here the grief and loss was something to be carried by many others, communally, even by people he hardly knew. It took a little getting used to.

This man was one of her uncles; he worked in a pump station. This one was her father's second wife's sister's son. That one used to work in security but he was now working with one of the sections in agriculture, and was her father's brother's nephew. His father had taken more wives after the one Khanyi grew up with, and their children were also her brothers and sisters.

She began explaining to him about small fathers and small mothers, and he thought he had worked out what these relations were, but her society and family connections were highly complicated. She knew an amazing number of women, all of whom were sisters, and they all wanted to meet him and chat.

There were distinct levels of people. Those she would ask him to stop for, so that she could greet, sometimes offering them a lift, and others who only merited a wave. Some subtle levels existed within the degree of closeness. There were proper somebodies and others who were something less than proper. Occasionally, she would wave weakly at someone but then dismiss them. 'Ha! That one is drinking too much,' or, 'That one has many boyfriends,' or even, 'That one, he never goes to church, not even at Easter'.

Matt began realising that the Khanyi he knew, Sis Khanyi, the beloved maid the Barton family employed, was only one part of her total being. She was also well known and liked in her own local community. He loved spending these times with her in the car, because she became more relaxed in his company and behaved more naturally with him. She came to life when talking animatedly to her friends.

There was a sense that under the sunshine, in the layers and intricate folds of this community, in the different pace of life he was feeling, there was something that he'd never experienced in England. He was conscious of the passage of time, and that he could not carry on indefinitely like this, but he didn't want to think about the flight back and especially of saying goodbye to her. His good intentions of phoning his work to advise them of the timing of his return had fallen by the wayside, and it was something he knew that he was putting off, reluctant to risk breaking the spell he felt himself falling under.

It was something of a shock to realise he had been out for almost a fortnight already, but that he felt in no hurry to leave. The house was large and comfortable, much more pleasant than his little semi-detached. In many ways it was better equipped than his own house. There was so much more to see and do, and he was aware that he was thinking about Khanyi differently. Thinking of her as someone he wanted to spend a lot more time with. He wanted to get to know her better. She was warm, friendly, kind and pretty, and he hadn't met anyone who was anything like her before. He knew her smell now, some light and floral scent that she always wore. Knew her footsteps.

She had often caught him watching her at odd moments, and they were beginning to feel an attraction to each other. A seed of an idea was planted, and he began to wonder if there was any work he could do to stay in Swaziland. From the first few days, when she had been so reserved, so distant and formal, she had changed subtly towards him and seeing her coming in each morning had become the high point of his day. Once she'd left each evening, he almost immediately missed her presence. He almost wished that the process of wrapping up the estate would take longer. Time was going too fast, but he knew he had to get back to work.

Khanyisile in her heart was starting to feel confused. She had never met a white man like this one before. He was respectful to her, he was of similar age and treated her as an equal and often asked what she would like to do, and he really listened to her. This puzzled her. But he also looked at her as if he were interested in her as a woman. She knew when his eyes were on her, and felt she knew why.

She no longer looked away when he spoke to her.

She loved being with him. He was funny, and he teased her very softly about things she did, making her laugh, and this made her feel warm inside. She looked forward to telling him things. He had stopped calling her SisKhanyi, and just called her Khanyisile now, or

Khanyi. It seemed like he didn't see her as a sister anymore. She had started to relax around him.

He used to call and show her things he had done, and he had gradually begun to fix many things around the house using the old tools from the garage. She knew he was very clever. When one of the bakkies couldn't start, he fixed it. He mended the grass cutting machine, the washing machine, the stove in her house, the electric lights outside. He fixed the fence. He repaired the shower. He stopped the toilet from leaking water. He repaired her kettle and seemed to be able to do many things.

He never asked for much from her but he liked drinking tea, a lot of tea, and every morning he ate cornflakes. Never anything else. He would eat a big bowl of them, sometimes even two! Some of the boxes had weevils, but she would sieve them out and he would still eat them! He often asked her to join him for lunch or supper and they would cook and eat together.

She sometimes would glance at him shyly, from under her eyelashes, even wondering secretly what it would be like to have a white boyfriend, but then she would remember he was going to go back soon, and she'd feel sad, wondering what was going to happen to her. He was slowly filling a place in her heart that had never been filled before.

Chapter 13

A PLAN HATCHED IN HIS MIND and one afternoon he said, 'Khanyi, look soon I'm going to have to go back to England again to my work. What about you and me going to the club to have dinner?'

She looked unsure. 'With me? you want us to go together to have some food?'

'Yes sure,' he said, 'why not? We've been working hard and you have helped me such a lot these past few days. Let's go out and get some nice dinner.'

Khanyisile had been there once or twice before, mainly as babysitter, but viewed the club as a den of sin where old white men drank, fought with their wives, shouted orders at the barman and became drunk.

She wasn't sure how to respond to this, knowing that their going out together would be noticed, but she also wanted to go with him. Besides, he had asked so nicely.

'I can be very happy to come,' she said.

Matt actually dressed up that evening, as best as he could from what was in his suitcase. He borrowed one of his brother's many jackets, a little too big for him.

Khanyi had never seen him wearing a jacket, and she herself looked stunning. She had some outfits that only came out for weddings or big events, and the blue dress she wore was figure hugging and transformed her into someone glamorous. She even wore heels. He was a bit taken aback and didn't know what to say without embarrassing her.

As they got into the pick up together he said, 'You look absolutely amazing, Khanyi,' and she smiled bashfully and thanked him. Her eyes were sparkling. Compliments like that didn't often come her way, and if they did they usually came with a proposal demanding sex.

They drove along dusty dirt roads running between fields of cane and old bushveld trees, sitting close together until they reached the club with the restaurant, and he made her sit down first, choosing a small table for two near the side of the room. She had become very quiet and shy and looked around nervously.

A waiter brought menus, took their order for drinks and Matt explained to her some of the dishes she wasn't familiar with. She was horrified to hear that any humans ever ate snails.

They ordered and chatted, he sensing she felt a little awkward being with him in a public place but proud of escorting someone so attractive. It never occurred to him that their respective races and their dinner date would be unusual. When the meals arrived, they were well prepared and better than anything they could make at home. They both enjoyed the food, commenting on how it had been cooked, and this somehow prompted an easier conversation. Matt ordered a local beer, she had a Sprite. She began to relax and talked a little about things at her home and people connected to the house, and funny things that the Barton family used to do.

As they finished, a different waitress came to clear away, a young, plump girl with a round moon like face, heavily made up, and an elaborate plaited hairstyle, silver and golden threads woven into the patterns.

There was a rapid exchange of siSwati between the two women. Soon it sounded heated. The waitress turned quickly and walked out with the dishes.

Khanyisile suddenly became upset and her eyes welled up with tears. She looked away. He was concerned, knowing he'd missed something, and asked, 'What's wrong, Khanyi? What's happened?'

She shook her head and simply asked, 'Please Matt, can we go now?'

It was the first time she had ever called him Matt.

He didn't understand but paid and they left promptly, driving back to the house almost in silence. She stared fixedly through the side window. The entire evening had somehow changed with that exchange.

He asked if she would like some tea and she came into the kitchen with him, the dogs all gathering round her, sensing that something bad had happened. He tried to joke with her and lift the mood, but the special feeling and quiet intimacy between them had evaporated. This time he made them hot drinks and made her sit in the lounge. After she'd had her first few sips she seemed to compose herself and he asked her gently, 'Khanyi, what happened back there?'

'Aish Matt, that woman working there, she said something very painful to me, very painful.'

He kept quiet and waited, then gently asked what had been said.

'She said I mustn't think I'm special because I'm with a white man. They can easily get Swazi women and they like sleeping with them.'

He was horrified. Angry for her sake, and horrified that anyone would address a guest like that. Furious and upset too that he had completely missed the undercurrents of a young, black, single woman going out with a young white man in that small tight knit community.

'What! She said that to you as she was clearing the plates?'

'Yes. She called me something that was not nice, Matt.'

He was furious. Livid and almost shaking with rage, he wanted to leave immediately to have it out with them, but she said the club would be closed by now. He tried to comfort her, but the evening was spoilt, the mood gone, and she went off to bed still upset and very quiet.

The next morning, without telling her where he was going, he drove back to the club at high speed, arrived just as it opened and demanded to see the manager. He was taken through to meet a tall, distinguished, extremely polite and well-spoken young Swazi man wearing a jacket and tie. With none of the usual greetings and pleasantries, Matt made it very clear in choice words what he thought of the waitress's comments, how angry he was and how upset his guest had been. He barely managed to avoid swearing. The club manager handled the issue very professionally. He was visibly annoyed too, apologised to Matt and asked that his apologies be extended to Khanyisile. He said action would be taken the same day. He said that the waitress Hlobsile was new and had come from Mbabane, and they'd had some problems with her.

Matt had calmed down a bit and explained who he was and what he was doing, and the manager politely ordered him coffee. He introduced himself more calmly to the restaurant manager, a Mr. Million. T. Simelane, conscious of doing everything Khanyi had taught him to do but back to front. He had forgotten to greet properly, or to really introduce himself, and had just dived bluntly in, straight into this angry conversation.

Simelane said in his soft lilting voice, 'I'm very sorry about this, Mr. Barton. I knew your brother and his family well. I also know sisKhanyi. I used to see them here on weekends and they were good people. She is a good person. There were two small children. But please, so I can apologise, will you come again before you go back, and have another meal, which the club will pay for?'

Matt accepted the apology and said he would try, but Khanyi would have to agree first.

Driving back afterwards, he began to realise there was far more weight to her simply accepting his invitation than he had realised. Everything and everyone was connected here.

Chapter 14

KHANYISILE HAD TOLD SEVERAL PEOPLE that Mr. Matt was good at fixing things, and in that community this news spread far and fast. One morning a battered bakkie arrived; she thought it might be from one of the small grower's farms. In the back they had loaded what looked like a broken tractor part. The old vehicle lurched to a stop at the gate and two men got out, a younger man staying with the van, too scared of the circling dogs to enter. This small delegation walked up to the house, but they stood a little distance away, frightened of the barking dogs. The elder of the two removed a much worn cap, revealing his greying hair, and began to wring it in his big hands as though it was wet.

Matt came out and met them, by now able to at least greet them both in passable siSwati, thanks to Khanyi's daily lessons.

'Mr. Barton we are from Nkomati Farms Coop. I am Timothy Ngomezulu, Chairperson. These are my associates from the committee. We have heard that you are very good in repairing, so we are asking if at all you can help us by repairing this piece which we have brought. We have got money to pay you for this.'

Matt had already investigated an old Lincoln welder and other equipment covered in dust in the back of the garage, and went with them to have a look at the item. The dogs all followed, as if they could also add value to the assessment.

A local mechanic had tried to repair a tractor's stub axle, doing more harm than good. The repair had failed and left behind layers of melted metal and very bad welding. He thought about the type of hardened steel, thought about what he had to hand, and quickly thought through a repair procedure.

'Okay, gents. Bring it to the back of the house and I will have a look at it, but you must leave it with me. I can't do this type of repair quickly and I will need to buy a few things.'

This news was greeted with cries of approval and gratitude. He didn't realise it, but this statement left them in no doubt that the young white man had already promised to repair their tractor axle. All of them had heard him.

The youngster drove around the yard, reversed in to the workshop area and, with the help of Ndepethe and their combined strength, they carefully dragged the heavy component out of the van. It was spotlessly clean and carefully wrapped in clean fertiliser sacking.

With much shouted advice and grunting, they carried it to an outside workbench, where Matt made them position it in such a way that he could inspect the broken section. It was an unusual break.

'How did this happen?' he asked.

'It means our driver was coming back at night and he never see a bad pothole when pulling a trailer,' Ngomezulu replied.

'The new axle is costing more than E11 700, which we cannot afford. Now the tractor is standing but we need to plough.' They shook their heads at this figure.

'Well, let me see what I can do,' said Matt.

'How much is it going to cost?'

'Well, let's first see if I can fix it properly, then we can see how much'

'Aaah, Mr. Barton, the problem is I need to know how much, in case we cannot afford.'

Matt thought quickly, not even knowing the prices of materials, but thought about some welding gas, some special rods, his time, some machining down afterwards, converting English prices into local currency.

He did a quick mental calculation and replied 'I think about three thousand three hundred Rand, but it won't be more than that.' This met with silence at first.

The three men responded to this by shaking their heads gloomily, and requested some time to think. As a cooperative, they needed to discuss this matter, and retired into the deep shade of a mango tree to consult, each sitting down easily, one leg extended, their hands clasped around the other raised knee. It was a weighty and lengthy consultation.

Ngomezulu had selected a curved stick which he used to make certain important points, noting their validity and doubts in the dirt and making little holes to identify the alternatives. Their expressions were deep, prolonged and serious. Their voices rose and fell in a low rumble as each member raised a new point, then the others would evaluate this view and deliberate over it with great gravity. Periodically, they would stop talking completely and just sit there silently, looking around solemnly and considering the complex matter.

Matt wondered if he had done something wrong but Khanyi came up and stood beside him, gently touching his arm. 'They have got some money, Matt, but they don't know you yet, and they are discussing if they should ask you to repair it or if they must go somewhere else.'

She added, 'The younger one he says he thinks you know, the other one he says you look too young to know such things and you don't even have some children.'

Then she went to make them tea.

It was difficult for him to understand, coming from a corporate world where such decisions are taken by accountants, but this was a process that took time and would only move at its own unhurried pace. Khanyi took the milky tea out to them on a tray with a large cream-coloured enamel pot. He watched in awe as the youngest man carefully added seven heaped spoons of sugar into his cup, a habit he had also seen in other countries. The tray was returned with the sugar bowl completely empty.

Ndepethe, he noticed, also went and joined them, but seated himself on a large stone some distance away, under the shade of a tree. The dogs sauntered over and lay down around him. He began rolling himself a formidable smoke using the inside lining of a cement packet, a small shred of newspaper, copious saliva and a large twist of brown, sun dried, home-grown tobacco, drawn from an ancient Boxer packet. As they deliberated in low tones, he lit up this thick hand rolled cheroot, and occasionally would interject loudly, bellowing comments and unsolicited advice at the three farmers. Sometimes almost disappearing behind clouds of fragrant smoke in between bouts of deep tubercular coughing.

'What's he shouting at them, Khanyi?'

'He tell them there is nobody in the country who can do this except you.'

Matt looked at her, a bit startled.

'But he's only just met me!'

'Now he says they mustn't take so much time discussing because you are very busy and it may happen another job comes since everyone knows you, even in the Transvaal and Natal, in Tanzania and the Free State they are asking for you already.'

Matt stared at her, too astonished by this to even respond.

'Now he says to them that it's a pity that they are deciding to make you angry because they are already stealing your time, and it's better they must take the broken axle and go back to the river in the bush since they are confused in their minds. Maybe they can return once again when they are clear.'

She covered her mouth and laughed softly.

'He's a very bad man, Ndepethe, but he likes you too much.'

'But I never said any of that, Khanyi, I never said anything!'

'Yes Matt, it's true you never say it, but he is telling them you are very clever. He says you are like a doctor, the price is cheap, and if they leave it here you are going to fix it perfectly.'

Matt shook his head, amazed. 'But Khanyi, he mustn't say that! I haven't even started yet. What if I can't do it?'

'Aah no, there's no problem, Matt. He told them he thinks he is already having about sixty-seven years, and has stayed very long in the world, much more than them, but he has never seen another person like you.'

Matt shook his head, but this last remark seemed to settle the issue.

The three farmers completed their earnest conversation, nodding heads sagely. They erased the marks in the dirt as if they had left secrets in the soil there, stood up together, dusted off their pants and returned slowly from the shade of the mango tree.

Mr. Ngomezulu announced, 'We are agreed about the price. Please fix it for us, Mr. Barton. We will come on Friday, if you can finish by then.'

At this the youngest of the three removed a plastic bag from his pocket with a large wad of grubby bank notes and began counting them out.

'No, Mr. Ngomezulu,' Matt said. 'You don't need to give me anything now. You can pay me when it's finished.'

They were delighted at this news.

They all shook hands and walked back to their bakkie, starting it up with a clatter and wildly shaking tailgate and then driving away, the youngest bellowing friendly insults back at the gardener.

This was to be the first paid work Matt ever did in the Kingdom. He wasn't to know it, but this single action was to make his name famous in a whole farming community.

Khanyi watched them go and said, 'There's no problem, Matt. They are going to come back and they will pay you.' She seemed to know this without question.

Chapter 15

KEENLY AWARE OF HIS LIMITED time, he had a closer look at what he had to hand, and what he still needed. He made a list of various special items and asked Khanyi where he could get them. She didn't know what any of them were but thought the only place was at the Sugar Mill stores, which kept all the things that their business needed, but he would have to get permission to buy from the store.

One of her other uncle's small brothers was employed at the Mill security, and they phoned him. After a long conversation covering several other friends and relatives, some of who were deceased, she eventually mentioned they needed the stores number, and she asked who Matt could speak to at the stores.

Matt was surprised at how much time the simple enquiry took, but before very long he was speaking to Mr. Amos Gule, who responded very formally but seemed helpful and knew exactly the special welding rods he needed, and had them in stock. There was a surcharge for non-company employees, which Matt agreed to pay. He made an arrangement for that afternoon and Khanyi said she knew a back road to the stores.

'I will look forward to our meeting, Mr. Barton,' said Amos gravely. 'I recall I met your brother, the late Mr. Patrick Barton. He was a well-known and respected somebody.'

Amos, head storeman, worked in a long gloomy shed with windows that were seldom opened and never cleaned, and ran a mechanical store in much the same way it had been set up when the British colonials established it in 1938. He proudly used the same old Cardex system and stock cards, did the same stock counts in the same order, and loved all the terminology that went with it. He had started work as a humble cleaner, then gradually made his way up to take charge of a big and well stocked mechanical store. Everything needed by the mill and its surrounding buildings and all the estates came through there, from steel stock, tyres, light bulbs, toilet paper, farm equipment spares and roofing sheets, to welding materials, paint, fertiliser, pipes, sprinklers and cement. It had several other sub sections in the area and several thousand line items.

Amos had a number of assistants whom he managed strictly, applying the same rigorous approach he had learned from a dour, pipe-smoking Scot, Ewan McTavish, who'd established the first store at the start of the war and had died of excesses of whisky, gin and malaria in the early seventies.

Amos relished the procedures, documentation, expenditure reports, the carbon papers, and he strongly resisted any moves to computerise the stores whenever these were mentioned, putting up any number of reasons why this would never work. He had resisted change for almost forty years. His world was one of journal entries and reversals, stock adjustments, credits, authorisations, receipts and files full of red stores requisition slips. He saw no need to change a system that was still working, and he knew where everything was. He had a deep-seated, innate distrust of computers.

Many of the original firms who exported stationery in the early days had long ceased trading. Brentworth and Timpson of Leicester, Steven Coles of London – Stationery Suppliers to the Colonies. He could still remember eagerly unpacking boxes from them in his youth, and hoarding the English newspapers they used as packaging to read later. They even smelt of a foreign land.

He was tall and slender, with long limbs and long fingers, and he emerged from the darkness like a wraith when Matt arrived, greeting him politely, his low voice issuing from a great height. He had worked under various expatriate accountants and a succession of procurement managers, for the most part bone dry individuals who'd avoided all colour in their conversation, and he had picked up certain of their mannerisms.

'Good afternoon, Mr. Barton. I hope you are enjoying your visit to the Kingdom,' he said seriously. 'And what items do you require?'

Matt explained, and Amos issued instructions, sending the young parts pickers in their brown dust coats scurrying off into the cobwebbed darkness. They returned and began making a small pile of the things he needed.

Amos gloomily informed, 'We are unable to supply these hydrogen rods in smaller quantities than packs of forty. Will that be acceptable?'

Matt was just delighted that they had so much of what he needed, and asked politely, 'Mr. Gule, can I pay with a card?'

'Most regrettably I do not currently have such modern facilities at my disposal, Mr. Barton. I am permitted to receive cash reimbursements or you may open an account, in which case we shall invoice you using the postal service.'

'Then I will pay cash, Mr. Gule'

'That will be very suitable. We are happy to be of service'

Almost all of Gule's clients were well known to him, colleagues who bought items at cost price plus a meagre 3% handling fee with virtual money, all charges being levied internally between departments. He enjoyed the novelty of dealing with a real life customer and attending to his needs personally, and they parted warmly.

Khanyi had respectfully remained outside, completing in greater detail the conversation she had started with her brother the security guard. Matt was given several assistants to help carry his purchases to the van, and he and Khanyi drove home together, sitting quite close on the bench seat when they gave lifts to people she knew. The young store assistants had shamelessly tried to propose love to her but she'd dismissed them with a stare as cold as glass.

He had found out from Amos that almost all specialised repairs were transported to South Africa, a costly and time consuming nuisance. The admin involved in the border crossing alone was complicated. There must be a need for someone to do the kind of work he could do in the area. His mind was buzzing, running fast and thinking of possibilities. Many of the local companies had to transport things to SA for specialised repairs, and this was a frequent occurrence and a great expense. He began to wonder if he could do some work there, much in the way his brother had, but offering practical help, covering more complex specialised repairs to machinery rather than consulting.

He began to wonder if he could slowly build up enough of a clientele there to keep him busy.

As soon as they got back, he started work on the axle, quickly realising he ought to have bought some protective clothing. He found an old dust coat and heavy gloves under some planks and started the dirty job of gouging out all the old welding with a cutting torch, creating a clean new surface to work with. The job was simple, like bread and butter to him, but he worked carefully and was still busy when Khanyi came to tell him it was nearly dark, and time to eat.

They had started having dinners together, an event they both looked forward to. She still found it fascinating and enjoyed just being with him, and he was teaching her to make some dishes that he knew well, other than chicken and rice.

He had found out that she did not have a boyfriend, because her pastor warned her that boyfriends were all agents of Satan, and she had found out that he was still single and had never been married. From what he could see, Satan seemed to feature prominently in Swazi culture.

He had put it off as long as he could but, knowing he must, he phoned his work the next morning. He had reached a point where everything he had to do from his side was done, and the administrative work now shifted to insurance companies and the high court to pronounce Patrick and his entire family formally dead, opening the way for the deceased estate to be settled and paid out. Completing his side of it came as a relief.

They had all seemed to make this process as long, painful and as difficult as they possibly could. He had found the thickly accented Afrikaans women hard to understand over the phone, and having to explain deeply personal and painful things many times over to each new person assigned to handling different aspects of the case was emotionally wearing. He began to detest these phone calls, always having to explain that he couldn't speak Afrikaans, and then having to go through the entire story again with yet another one of their 'highly qualified agents who will be pleased to assist you', all of whom were equally ignorant and unhelpful. He was glad that part of the process was over.

He got through to Emma first, chatted to her briefly and asked to speak to the boss.

'Morning Mr. Pearson, it's Matt here, Matt Barton.'

'Aah, morning Matt. We've been wondering when you would surface. I was thinking of sending out a rescue party!'

'Yes sir, I'm sorry about this, it's all taken a lot longer than I thought it would.'

'Call me Brian, Matt, do call me Brian,' the director said generously. 'Now then, when are you planning on returning, lad? We need you back here.'

'Well uhmm, Mr. Brian, I uhmm was thinking if I could start back next Monday, fly back over the weekend?'

His inflection rose towards the end of the request, as if the tone would convey him asking if this would be alright. That was still three more working days away.

Brian was already fending off Kuwait, who had asked for Matt specifically and by name, and the Tomsk Refinery work that needed him too, but they would probably cope till then.

‘Alright, Matt, I think we can do that. Let’s make it Monday. We look forward to having you back, but you’ll have to hit the ground running. How are you finding the place? What was it again… Swazi something?’

‘Swaziland, sir, I’m in Swaziland. Well, it’s very different. People have been very kind about the whole thing. It’s a bit hard to explain what it’s like here.’

‘Well good, good’ – not wanting to get into details – ‘as long as you’re wrapping things up, we certainly need you back here, the Arabs and the bloody Russians are both asking for you already, I must rush. I’m due at some blessed EU IME Fabrications Standards Session in Paris in a few hours. God knows why, but they’ve gone and made me president. Safe flight back, Matt, see you soon.’

He pictured busy, kindly and clever Mr. Pearson behind his huge desk, the stunning Emma faithfully sitting outside, organising his flight and chivvying, urging him out and towards his driver.

He rang off, somehow feeling as though something alien had passed through the phone, a whiff of intense activity. A taint of the hectic, busy, global life and many demands he had been used to. An odd realisation quickly followed that he had not really missed being away from it. He had sailed close to the centre of the whirlpool, but steered out of it again.

There were so many other things to occupy his mind here. Firstly Khanyi, whose presence and absence had begun filling his waking thoughts, and secondly a broken tractor axle. His late brother’s estate had been given a different priority, and his UK welding job had moved even further down the order. It was an odd feeling, after having put his work first for so many years, and having had the burden of the estate sitting on him so heavily. Something had subtly changed within him, but he couldn’t identify it.

He looked out of the study windows onto the smooth lawns, the neatly trimmed beds and trees, and the motley assortment of dogs roaming around after Ndepethe, and was suddenly struck by the depth of the legacy his brother had created. There was a whole history here that would come to a stop if he sold the home and went back to England.

Matt never put on any front. He noticed neither colour nor class and took people for what they were. The realisation that his brother had been well off, well settled and had left him a very substantial estate had forced him to think about things differently. He had thought he was just coming out to wrap up a small household, as quickly as possible, then would return to the job he thought he loved, but he hadn't expected to encounter his growing feelings for Khanyi.

He had sort of imagined them all living in a rough little place in the bush. He hadn't thought she would be like she was, and had never thought it would be like this.

As he walked back to the workshops, he realised that he missed her whenever she was away, and that the times she would come up to wherever he was, either just for a chat or to ask him something, or to tell him there was a call or even bring him a cup of tea, were the high points of the day. She occasionally touched his hand or shoulder to show him something and this had thrilled him.

As he opened the taps on the cutting torch and set the flame to begin preheating the repair area, he thought of their little dinners together. They had been some of the happiest times of his life. He loved the way she smiled, the way she moved, her hands, her short little pony tail and the way she talked. He enjoyed watching her doing the simplest of things, like feeding the dogs or answering the phone. She had a timeless grace that he could not quite describe when she moved.

He was fascinated by the colour of her skin, which was neither brown nor black, but a kind of light coffee colour that he wanted to touch and feel.

He was beginning to feel that, more than anything else, he just wanted to be with her, see her every day and talk to her about everything. He had never before thought about anything else when he was working, but now found it hard to concentrate. His mind was carrying two thoughts: the right flame colour for preheating high grade steel before high strength welding, and what he and Khanyi would have for supper and how soon she would come out with a drink so he could stop and tell her what he was doing. It was a new sensation for him.

There was sunshine here, there were good people, and he began to see that in this world there were proper somebodies and other kinds of people who weren't proper somebodies. It was a complicated but clear distinction.

Everyone said 'Hau!' when they were surprised, and he had started to say this himself.

There was warmth and a closeness he had never felt before. Some of it had worn off on his brother and Mel; they were different too. It was as though they carried something smouldering in their hearts that stayed alight, even when they were away from home, and he was beginning to feel it in himself. When they phoned SisKhanyi, the flame would be stoked high again, and Melanie especially would always return glowing and beautiful from the phone with some home news: the litchis were in fruit, Shogun had caught a leguaan, and the ridgebacks had caught three guinea fowl but eaten two before Ndepethe could retrieve them. The night watchman at the compound had caught a thief and had beaten him.

It was colourful.

He had been unable to really understand it then, but was beginning to feel it now.

The metal was beginning to glow a dull red and he began steadily moving the torch to preheat, wary of the steel losing its temper and weakening.

Chapter 16

Coming back into the house later that day he thought he heard crying. He followed the soft sound and opened the door to what had been the children's shared bedroom. Khanyi was sitting on the bed, holding a little girl's dress, with neat piles of children's clothes around her. She was weeping softly and looked up at him with reddened eyes, clutching the red and blue frock as though her life depended on it.

'I wanted to tidy up their clothes, Matt, but when I saw Jackie's dress I remembered, I mean I didn't… I couldn't finish here. It is painful because I can see the children in their clothes. She used to love this dress. Every day, every day she wanted to wear it, now she can't, she can never…'

He stepped quickly over to the bed, reached down and lifted her from it. She came into his arms and he stood, still dirty from his work, and hugged her tightly. He drew in some of her pain and loss and felt her body gradually softening and easing into his, and she hugged him back. Their faces were very close and he could feel her sweet breath on his face, but she was still crying and sniffing and kept her eyes away from his.

'We've lost such special people. It will always hurt us, Khanyi, but one day it won't hurt as much as it does now. I promise you, it will get better.' He soothed her, gently rubbing her shoulders, smoothing her hair. She trembled and he felt her shaking.

'When I see the clothes I can see the children, Matt, and then it makes me too sad.'

'I know you loved them. They were like your children too, and they both loved you, Khanyi, they loved you so much. They always talked about you whenever they talked about home.'

She looked up at him, surprised

'Hau! Matt, they told you about me, even in England?'

'Always, Khanyi, every time. Whenever I saw them they used to tell me about you. The songs you taught them, the sweet buns you used to buy for them, the way you washed them in the bath, how you got the little one to sleep even if he was upset. The special way you made rooibos tea for them. They always wanted to buy you presents. They really loved you.'

She burst into tears again at this, but somehow looked different. There was something he had said that she drew comfort from, even in her loss.

After a little while she composed herself, caught her breath and drew slightly away from him.

'I don't know what must I do with their things, Matt. Must I pack them?'

'You know what, Khanyi? Let's just leave everything in their room exactly as it is for now. There's no hurry. When you feel ready, we can decide what to do. It's too soon for now.'

The family's presence was still very strong in the children's room, even a hint of a smell, and just being there had brought it all to the surface again.

He wished he knew how to ease her pain, but it was still too deep and too recent, and he somehow knew it was too soon without realising it. He was glad he had been there for her.

They both missed them. Apart from the children, he had lost his only brother and a friend, and Khanyi had lost a family.

He returned to his work, drawing on his training and many years' experience of difficult repairs. He easily slipped into the role again. Much of what he had to do was familiar, almost instinctive. A small adjustment to the current, a subtle alteration in his hand position, always watching the molten pool and not the white-hot arc itself, as he had been taught as a young man.

He was a master of his trade, and either worked as near to perfection as anyone could, or not at all. In this guise, all his skills were in use, and he was in his element. The careful layers of weld grew, cooled and strengthened the repair, despite the age of the welding machine.

He welded with such precision that, as he slowly worked his way around and across the awkward crack, smoothly changing his hand position, the slag layer curled and lifted off cleanly as it cooled, leaving a perfectly clean surface for each successive layer. He could visualise the molten steel penetrating deep into the crack as he welded and he knew what was going on deep inside the steel.

He knew that it would be a successful repair because he knew exactly what he was doing, and had done it expertly. His actions were unhurried and practised, and he poured his own strength and sense of loss into the repair. It would stay welded once he had repaired it.

The power tripped often, or the old machine would overheat, and he would stop, take a break and look around, almost in disbelief at where he was working. Instead of being under artificial lights, deep in the gloomy dripping pillars of some orange-painted North Sea oil rig, surrounded by cursing oil riggers and their piles of porn DVDs, he was looking out at dappled sunshine on green lawns, ancient trees standing undisturbed beside neat flower beds, dogs basking in the sun or chasing lizards, depending on their breed and, above it all, the exciting reassurance that if he wanted to, he could go inside and talk to Khanyi and she would smile and talk back. He knew clearly which was better for his soul. He could sell his skills for more money, stash it unspent in his account and live like a global blacksmith, or abandon the dollars and the flights and live like a proper person with a life.

Maybe a life with her...

A light, inaudible breeze stirred the high branches in the trees around him and he suddenly sensed again his brother's close proximity in the peaceful cleanness of that garden.

The air seemed to be humming, alive with something that he felt intensely but could not describe or see. He could feel his heart pumping inside his chest and his nerves making him tremble. He remembered talking in the hire car, as he drove along barely three weeks ago. 'Pat,' he murmured to himself, 'should I stay here and make a new life? Am I doing right by you...Would it work out?'

Sensing the subtle change in atmosphere in the way that domestic animals often will, three of the largest dogs rose from where they lay, wagged their tails and walked lazily towards him, watching his face closely, their wheaten bodies swinging easily as they moved. One licked at his hand, then all three walked round and round several times in small circles before lying down, literally at his feet, the biggest male dog laying his broad head and heavy forequarters right on one of his feet.

He could feel the dog's warmth through the leather and stood motionless, surrounded by the big, affectionate animals. Dogs who had accepted him as a substitute master, and had become loyal companions, guarding him forever more, with their lives if need be. Patrick had always loved dogs, always wanted packs of them about the place. There was always at least one terrier that never left his side, and Mel teased him about it and the way he spoilt her. She even attended business meetings with him and regularly visited the bank, trotting up to the counter with her master like a valued customer. The little female had transferred her affections to Khanyi almost entirely, and merely tolerated Matt.

Maybe the Barton dogs were giving him the answer he was searching for. If he made a single move, did anything at all, his action would immediately trigger a mighty din of long tails banging on the floor, tapping against the welding machine, whipping against the bench. The only way they could get any closer to him would be by climbing inside his dust coat. They couldn't speak, but they gazed at him seriously, watching his every move and guarding him from harm. They had become his dogs now. It was going to be hard to leave them.

He finished the lengthy repair and, after it had cooled, began laboriously grinding and polishing the steel, creating a smooth new shoulder for the wheel bearing. He didn't have access to a lathe, but was skilled enough to file and polish away steadily at the steel with hand tools and, by measuring often, he created a surface that would be good enough for the seal.

You could not see the repaired section of axle steel any more. The new metal had completely blended with the old and it all looked like one piece, which was as he wanted it. The repair was seamless.

Eventually, he was satisfied with its dimensions, finish and accuracy, given the tools he had, and he coated the gleaming steel with clean grease, wrapped it back in its fertilizer sacking and waited for them to collect it.

On Friday afternoon, his last remaining weekday, the battered old bakkie arrived, rattling and shaking, carrying the same three passengers. They came in, examined his handiwork and were amazed.

'Hau! But it looks like new!' Mr. Ngomezulu exclaimed.

They all stood around admiring the repair. The youngster drew out his familiar dirty plastic shopping bag and began counting out money, and, as they had requested an invoice, Matt printed one using Galloway Consulting stationery. It came to a little less than his estimate because he had used fewer welding rods and gas, and he invoiced them the reduced total.

The old gardener wandered up and called something at them, laughing to himself and inducing another long spasm of coughing. Khanyi explained, 'He says he told them that you are a doctor. He told them you will fix this perfectly. He is laughing because he says they must never forget he is older than all of them so he knows things they still don't know.'

The representatives from Nkomati Farms were very grateful. They thanked him for the repair and told him that in future they wouldn't try to fix such things themselves, but bring them straight to him. He didn't have the heart to explain that he might not be there next time, but he was confident that the repair would hold, and that they would be able to get the tractor working again.

They all lifted together, reloaded the heavy item and then drove off, waving happily back and thanking him profusely. Suddenly the vehicle braked and swerved to a sudden halt some distance away. The youngest of the three leapt out and ran back to the house carrying a small sack.

'Sorry, Mr. Barton, we brought this for you from the farm. I forget to give you; it is a present from Nkomati Farms Cooperative to thank.'

He handed over the sack to Matt, who noticed that the dogs were all very interested in its contents. It contained a live brown chicken that looked up through the open bag at him with beady eyes and clucked contentedly. The youngster jogged back to rejoin his associates, leapt agilely into the back, and then they drove off, leaving dust hanging in the still evening air.

'What should I do with this hen?' he asked Khanyi.

'We can eat it now, or give it to Ndepethe. He has got many chickens at his home'

Matt called the old man across and gave him the African gift, and thanked him for his help.

'Tell him he is a very good marketing manager,' he told Khanyi, smiling to her as he said it.

The old man thanked him and announced that it would produce many chicks so he would not kill it. It was a special bird because it brought money to the house. He would call it Nkomati.

There was no argument to that.

Chapter 17

THAT EVENING, KHANYI NEEDED TO visit some family members who had suffered a death, but she promised to return early on Saturday morning. He needed to leave by midday to catch the Jo'burg flight, and time suddenly seemed to be running away from him. The morning began to cloud over and a chill wind started blowing gustily out of the south. It grew in intensity and doors and windows started slamming in the house. He was already packed, but there were many things still left outside from the repair. He rushed around tidying these away and stashing them under shelter, and Khanyi returned just in time to join in closing the windows and doors and hurrying to bring in clean linen off the line.

'Yoh! It is going to rain, Matt. It is going to rain just now! We must hurry.'

He helped her by quickly folding up the sheets and towels, but they got caught in it, the first big cold drops hitting the ground and splattering hard against them. The rain stung against their skin and wetted them.

It started intermittently but quickly turned into a downpour, a torrent of heavy, drenching, cold rain that had come out of nowhere. In African rain storms you can get soaked very quickly.

They ran into the kitchen, both wet and laughing, and he took one of the clean towels and began to dry the droplets of rain off her hair and face, as they stood close together.

'You must change, Matt,' she said. 'You can't go wearing wet clothes on the aeroplane. You will get sick!'

She took the towel from him and reached up on her tiptoes, trying to wipe off his head and face, and he saw the rain had soaked her clothes and made her blouse see-through. She felt his eyes on her breasts but had to stand even closer to reach his hair and he gently took her hand and drew it away from him. He could see tiny rain drops on her eyelashes and cheeks, and silver droplets on her hair and neck, and, as she raised her head as if to enquire why he had taken her hand, he kissed her. They kissed tentatively at first, as though unsure of each other's feelings, and then more deeply.

He felt her body growing soft against his, and her wet breasts pressing against his chest, and she kissed him back, sighing softly with pleasure.

She had first thought, this is wrong, I cannot be doing this, but then her longing for him overwhelmed her and the kiss pushed everything else out of her mind and she kissed him back. She felt as though she were melting into him and sliding downwards.

They stood there, wet and very close, with a heightened awareness of each other's bodies but also knowing that time was running out and he had to leave. He put both hands around her slender waist and pulled her in, becoming aroused at her physical closeness.

They kissed again.

After a little time they drew apart, and he smiled.

'I've been wanting to do that for a long time.'

'I know.'

'If you knew then why didn't you…'

She put her finger on his lips. 'Shhh, I had to first know you were going to come back.'

'Do you know it now?'

'Yes I think so.'

'I am, Khanyi, I am coming back. I wanted to explain but we never talked about. I mean, we never, we haven't, I didn't know if…'

'I know.'

'Khanyi, we're out of time now but I must go back to England to tell them that I want to leave. I am going to come right back here. I want to be with you. I want you with me all the time. I hate to go and I'm sorry it's like this but I will come back, I promise.'

'I understand, Matt. You are going to finish that side then you will come back here. I'm going to wait for you. You'll find me here, together with the dogs and the house.'

'I think I love you, Khanyi. I just couldn't find the right time to tell you.'

Her eyes filled with tears

'I also love you, Matt. I am going to miss you too much now.'

They kissed once more, more relaxed with each other by now, and she pressed herself up against him, slightly moving her legs apart, her sweet breath close to his face. One tension had left them but had been replaced by another more intense one.

He thought how lovely she looked and how white her teeth were.

It was all happening now, with exquisitely bad timing, but he was clear in his mind. He was going to resign, he was going to phone her every week he was away, and he was coming back to her as soon as possible. This place was going to become home, with her in it.

Everything had changed.

'You must phone me, Matt. Please phone me sometimes.'

'I will. Wherever I am I will phone, and I'll miss you all the time.'

He quickly unpacked a clean shirt, rubbed himself dry and changed. They shared one last kiss together, different to the others, and he threw his bags into the hire car and started back to the airport, skidding and splashing through the puddles like a rally car.

The rain had stopped and he wound down the car window. The air outside had changed. It smelt fresh and clean, an invigorating smell of wet trees and broken leaves. He had never felt more certain of anything in his life. Everything had changed.

The drive back to the airport felt different to him, and the process of checking in and leaving for Johannesburg was straightforward.

He went through the motions automatically, his mind far away from travelling. The small jet took off and Matt idly watched as the ground fell away, the rain easing now with the bushveld trees and game trails fading into deep shadows, but it all felt different. Far away to the east, in the direction of the smoke from the sugar mill and a range of blue hills, he thought of Khanyi, busying herself with feeding the dogs and cooking her own supper. The rain had washed the air clean, and he could see almost to the horizon and the Indian Ocean.

Matt wondered what she was thinking at that moment, and if she was thinking about him too.

The aircraft gradually levelled off and after a short while he could no longer see the Lebombo Mountain range, as darkness began to creep into the shadowed purple valleys behind him.

Landing and transiting in the modern, brightly lit, busy airport outside Johannesburg was quick, and he found himself in a business lounge, checked in and waiting for his main flight north, back to England. Before, he had always felt a vague satisfaction at this last stage of a trip, knowing that he was heading back to what was familiar, leaving behind him his reputation and a repair well completed.

This time he couldn't stop thinking about her, wondering when he would speak to her again and trying to understand the feeling. He wanted to see her again and to hear her voice.

They boarded and were served dinner and eventually he slept, and was gently awakened several hours later by one of the immaculately groomed air crew, going through the cabin with quiet efficiency, tidying away blankets and empty bottles. She asked, 'Good morning, sir, would you like an *English* breakfast.' He smiled at the familiar accent.

When the big jet had come to a standstill, as soon as they opened the hatches a wet, leafy smell flooded into the cabin, green and damp and unique to England, but it didn't fill him with the usual sense of belonging.

He found the trip home and his reintroduction strange.

It seemed odd that people didn't greet each other, they didn't thank each other and, when he automatically said 'Hau!' in surprise at the delayed departure time for his Northbound train, someone turned and commented sarcastically, 'How? How? It's not rocket science mate. The bloody train's late innit? Leaves on the track. I saw it on me mobile!'

He took a taxi home, using a familiar Polish driver he had often used before at the beginning and end of long trips, and opened up the front door to his cold home, turning on some lights, the heating and the geyser. It was deathly quiet and very cold in the hall.

The fridge was empty but for half a tomato on a plate and some very sour milk.

Chapter 18

ARRIVING BACK AT WORK ON Monday morning was like trying to get onto an escalator that was already moving at great speed. Everyone seemed to be very busy, everything was urgent and, although people were glad to see him, their greetings were hurried and superficial because they were all rushing to do something. He went upstairs and saw Emma, asking her to tell Mr. Pearson he was back.

She smiled and looked at him, fluttering her long eyelashes. 'How did you go, Matt? Everything alright over there?'

'Thanks, Emma. Yeah, I guess it went okay. It's all a bit complicated though.'

'Well, I'll tell Brian. He'll be well pleased. He's been asking for you but he's in Frankfurt until Wednesday.'

Matt logged on to his worksite and checked his schedules, finding he was already booked to fly out the next morning to Achinsk, east of Kazakhstan, to carry out some emergency repairs at an oil refinery. It was a flight of three legs, each one in a smaller aircraft. He went down to the stores and found his friend Salikh.

'Eh up Matt, are yer right? I've not seen yer for a good bit.'

'Aye, not so bad Salikh. How're you doing?' He slipped easily back into the regional accent, in Salikh's case a mixture of broad Lancashire and British Pakistani.

'Well, we 'ave missed yer, pal. They sent young Andy to finish that seawater plant in Dubai, on them stainless induction pipes and flanges, but he made a right dog's bollocks of it. They had to go back with a team.'

Matt knew what that meant.

It was what the specialist welders and metal workers wanted to avoid at all costs. If the job wasn't done properly and anyone ever had to go back, any further costs after the initial work completion were to the firm's account. Sending a team almost always meant an enquiry and some very unpleasant meetings. In some cases it meant a disciplinary hearing for the unfortunate employee. The welders seldom spoke about it at work and all hated going back.

It had happened to Matt once, when he was quite new and inexperienced. He had carried out a repair in India and used the wrong settings, believing the material to be what he had been told it was but not testing it for himself, and two of his own welds failed under pressure, after he had returned to the UK. Somewhere deep in his personnel file there was a first written warning about the event.

He knew Andy slightly and felt sorry for him.

'Otherwise, what's up?'

'Well, Mr. Brian's been looking for yer, and we've got a new multipurpose MIG machine in. Oh aye, and Emma reckons that fit wench with the big boobs and green hair in the canteen is having twins. She's fockin huge!'

They began talking about people and work. Salikh was right up to date with technology and always willing to talk shop to the technicians. He had to ensure that the welders had the best possible equipment for different situations, and often arranged training for them on new techniques. In his daily dealings he had learnt a lot about the kind of work they did, and the unique welding problems they sometimes faced.

'I'm off to Achinsk tomorrow. Chat again then, Salikh.'

'Oh yer, there again are ye? What've them Cossacks buggered now? Let's hope you don't have to stay in that hostel with them cats like last time. I'll get a travpack ready for you.'

'I'd forgotten about them. I hope not. Cheers then.'

He knew it was always cold where he was going and left work early to pack special clothing, beginning to feel tired from the overnight flight. Salikh had provided him with what they called a travel pack, a few special tools and testing equipment that would help him to evaluate the material, determine the specific kind of repair and establish exactly what was needed. It was hard to think about when he would call Khanyi, when he would get a chance to see Mr. Pearson and the looming Achinsk refinery repair all at once.

Within days, Matt was back living his old life, a bit jetlagged, crawling painfully through a narrow space in a maze of steel piping to reach the awkward site of a cracked flange coupling, rejoining heavy pressure pipes that normally carried super-heated steam. It was very cold in the plant and the work lamp they provided was flickering and dim. He was staying at a worker's hostel in Krasnoyarsk nearby. It was basic but adequate, and he knew from previous trips there would be a night frost. The wild cats would be yowling with cold and passion during the night.

He tried to explain to the stern faced woman who ran the hostel with an iron rod, stamping around in heavy brown stockings and muttering to herself, that he didn't want butter in his tea, but when he declined the pungent pickled carp and onions for breakfast, this had annoyed her. He settled for unleavened black bread and hard boiled eggs. Khanyi, Ndepethe, the farm house, sunshine and the dogs seemed a million miles away. He hadn't been able to tell anyone about what had happened on his trip, and desperately wanted to explain it.

He could see her face, her smile and her bright eyes, a bit like a cat, turning from the stove to laugh with him at one of the dogs, and thought of her sitting next to him watching TV. Images of her face, her soft lips and the feel of her waist in his arms kept coming into his mind. It was oddly different. Somehow things were lighter, as though all that he was feeling and everything around him was very temporary. The rooms were either overheated or freezing, and communication was difficult, but he took it all calmly. She was there, and she was waiting for him and he could imagine her.

He made his regular phone call to Salikh and ordered everything he would need. The storeman offered to send a water pistol for the feral cats.

After work the next evening he called the house number in Swaziland. He wasn't sure of the time difference. The phone rang for a long time and then Khanyi answered, sounding breathless, as though she had run in from the garden.

'Hello, this is the Barton's house. It's Khanyisile speaking.'

'Hi, Khanyi, it's Matt.'

'Hau, Matt! Hello! Hello, Matt how are you? Where are you? Are you okay?'

He loved the sound of her voice. She sounded excited to hear him.

'Sorry if I woke you. Yes, I'm fine. I'm in Russia, very far away, and it's very cold here. How is everything there?'

'Aah, we are fine, but it is also a bit cold. Ndepethe says he heard that tractor is still fine. He said they want to bring a plough and a water tank when you come back.'

'That's good, that's good to hear. And how are you doing?'

'No, I'm fine Matt but I miss you too much! It's quiet here now. When will you come back?'

Her voice was soft and he loved hearing her soft African accent again.

'As soon as I can, Khanyi. I have to see the boss first, but I'll see him when I get back this week, I promise, and then I'll tell you. What's the time there now?'

'It's in the afternoon, Matt. I was picking some vegetables before. At first I never hear the phone. But I don't mind. Please come soon, Matt, but we are all fine here.'

She sounded a little tearful.

'I miss you every day, all the time.'

'I miss you too.'

The radio phone connection then started to squawk and howl and he rang off. He looked around at the pale green walls, the heavy, dark wooden furniture, the hideous yellow linoleum flooring and the seventies orange and brown geometric patterned bedspread, and wondered about what new horror would be served for dinner. He smiled, thinking about hearing her voice again and wondered what she wore in bed.

Tomorrow, hopefully the gear should arrive, then maybe on Thursday he could start repairs. Friday night he should get home, and maybe get to see Brian, but he doubted it. There were local flights involved and none of the domestic carriers were reliable time keepers. The aircraft usually looked old and often broke down. If worst came to worst, he would have to phone him and explain, but he didn't want to have that conversation over a phone.

He washed his face and went down the cold steel stairs to brave what was being served for the evening meal. There were several young men staying in the hostel, reserved but quite friendly, but they only spoke Russian and some Finnish. One of them knew a few words of English and, using this and the universal sign language for a pint, indicated that they wanted to invite him to come out with them for a drink. Matt agreed and, after dressing for the cold, they all stepped out together into the evening.

They strolled along quickly, smoking, chatting and laughing together, he wishing he could follow their rapid conversation. Their workboots crunched on the thin ice covering puddles along the roadside. There was little traffic and they walked abreast. The bar was smoke-filled, plain and cheap, with wooden tables covered in red and white plastic print, mainly there to serve serious drinkers. It had the same pale blue paint decorating the windows that he had noticed on other buildings and the orthodox churches. A widescreen TV in the corner, secured in a steel cage, was showing an ice hockey game. Matt noticed a few young women decoratively placed at various tables, mostly without apparent partners, and they sneaked long hungry looks at the young foreigner whose looks and clothing gave him away.

Matt and Patrick had been a similar size, strong but not heavily built, and the brothers were often mistaken for Irishmen, with dark hair and heavy eyebrows, pale skin, and a coal pile beard that grew quickly. By the evening of every day Matt needed to shave and he knew he needed one now, but his beard made him look like a rugged actor with designer stubble. Most of the lads with him were solid, round faced, rosy cheeked and fair haired and he stood out among them. They drank a weak dark beer with vodka chasers, and Matt paced himself carefully, matching one drink to their three, knowing from previous visits that he would not last the night.

After a few hours of politely smiling at their jokes, breathing their smoke, and trying to follow some of the conversation, and after having bought a few rounds for the youngsters, he politely made his excuses, miming his need for sleep, and left for the hostel, just as two of the bolder girls, made up and dressed to kill, hitched up their skirts and decided to come and join their table. They were disappointed.

Chapter 19

MEANWHILE, BACK IN SWAZILAND KHANYISILE had decided to use some of her inheritance on some modern new clothes. She wanted to look different when Matt came back, and had decided she was no longer willing to wear clothes suited only for church or for work. She drew some cash, took a fast bus to Manzini and spent a happy day walking around and buying clothes, visiting store after store. It was the first time in her life she had ever bought clothes for cash, shopping without having to count every cent and worry constantly about how much she could afford to repay. She was enjoying the independence of shopping for more than one item at a time, and having enough money to pay for her choices.

Khanyi had lived frugally and worked hard for most of her life. She was slim and pretty, with a high, slender waist, one of those lucky women on whom new clothes seem to fit easily. She didn't have to find what fitted her; she could easily choose between many clothes that all fitted her perfectly.

When someone looking like that walks into ladies' outfitters with the clear intention of spending money, any properly trained assistants leap into action. She knew the look she wanted to achieve, and would not be side tracked by other ideas.

The young female staff, sensing an imminent sale, brought her armfuls of inappropriate, trashy colours and revealing clothing, but after visits to several different shops, and feeling very daring, she settled on some branded jeans that fitted her perfectly, several light new blouses, a few new sun dresses, new underwear and some loose fitting tops. She wanted to stop looking like a domestic worker but didn't want to look cheap. She had an innate sense of style and taste that was instinctive, and chose clothes that were young and complimented her.

She had never actually worn jeans before – her pastor warned all the church women against doing so – but she often saw the younger white wives, younger teachers and some secretaries working at the mill wearing them. She thought they looked smart and sexy, even though she had been told they were sinful.

Her new jeans made her feel smart and independent, and she even treated herself to KFC for lunch, something she could never normally afford. Even with the new shoes, she had hardly made a dent in the money they had left her, and she came home on the bus sleepy, happy and excited by her new purchases. It was a wonderful experience, shopping for things that made her look good instead of things that were affordable, would last many washes, and were modest enough to meet the approval of the elders.

She knew that the elders would not approve of her becoming involved with Matt. He was white, and he didn't attend their church, and he had not been pre-approved by them, but a long subdued rebelliousness in her made her feel that she wanted to be with him anyway. She had never felt the way she'd felt when he was staying at the house and she wanted to feel it more, and feel it more intensely. She wondered if this was what being in love meant. She knew that in time he would want to sleep with her, but thought that he would not force her to do it, and although she felt nervous about being with him, she looked forward to it more.

She decided it would not be possible for her to continue going to her old independent church group. The pastor would make her stand up and confess, and the elders would be cross with her for the sin of wearing the wrong clothes – clothes that showed off her shoulders, her long legs or her figure. They would publicly admonish her and make her cry.

This problem nagged at her conscience as the bus travelled slowly back down to the lowveld. It dropped her off at a small market place near the house and she walked back home as it grew dark, carrying all her bags, wondering if God was also cross with her and with Matt.

Chapter 20

MATT, DEEP IN THE HEART of Russia, was finding that nothing goes according to plan when there is a long international supply chain involved. Some of the equipment arrived intact, but a small crate with a special inverter and cable extensions had been freighted to an airport in Finland, and trying to recover it proved very difficult.

He couldn't start work without it. He turned to the refinery engineering manager Palamachev for help, who was spitting mad and proceeded to have a growling, furiously angry argument with the Moscow forwarding agent who had misdirected the shipment. It meant waiting another day.

Eventually, the equipment arrived. He crawled painfully into position and started and, after a long day's work, stiff and weary, coughing from the fumes, he finally finished the repairs but stayed to watch them tested under working pressure the following morning. He finally left Achinsk on Saturday, just managing to catch an earlier afternoon flight and facing a series of delayed connections.

These things were so common that previously they hadn't upset him, but he wanted to give Brian Pearson a proper month's notice, and was feeling every additional day he was away from Khanyi very deeply. It almost hurt to think about her.

He finally got home to his own house again and unlocked his front door on Sunday evening, after a wearisome day and a half spent travelling, dozing fitfully in airport seats and lounges, watching endless reruns of the same news, being placed on standby for different flights and snacking on odd meals from strange containers at odd times. He was very tired and the time felt wrong.

Matt seldom dreamt, and when he did he seldom remembered his dreams, but in the early hours of that dark morning he had a terrifying dream, waking up with a start, sweating and shouting. His own cries had woken him up and, thrashing away at an unseen enemy, he had thrown off all the bedclothes and was cold and wet with sweat.

He switched on the bedside lamp and lay awake, his heart beating so fast that he could feel it inside him. He tried to work through the mist of what had just happened and it came flooding back.

There was a huge lion, determined to kill him but, in the way of dreams, it had chased him through different cities and places where he had worked, even wandering into different countries. It was lying in wait under the walkway he lay on as he welded in Achinsk, then he had down turned into a side street he knew was in Madrid, rid of it at last, and it was on the pavement, massive, scarred and tawny grey, staring straight at him with its ferocious eyes glaring, utterly cold and filled with hatred. It kept hiding behind things he vaguely knew, like an access path in Egypt, when it had appeared silently from behind a silo in a refinery, then it came and stood above him on a catwalk, looking down and watching him. Then, as he panicked, the lion became three, and they were swimming, circling black shark fins somehow swimming around in a garden as he floundered in the sea and desperately tried to get away.

There was safety at the top of a ramp, a crudely built loading platform, steeply sloped with reinforced concrete sides. It was backfilled with earth, with steel rings set in the wall. If he could only reach it – he had to get to it and get out of the water and away from the sharks – but they became lions again as they set foot on the ground, watching him like prey with their unblinking golden eyes. He could smell the big cat scent on them.

He swam frantically for the loading ramp but they were quicker, then he made landfall and ran up it, desperately shouting at them to keep away, but they became dogs with lion faces and fangs. Big shaggy dogs with brindle coats but lion faces. As he came out of the water, he knew they would catch him and devour him unless he jumped, and the high end of the ramp looked down onto a peaceful scene of acres and acres of tall standing crops, deep green, even and gently moving in the breeze, with a smell coming from the fields that he recognised. The walls of the platform had become a mighty cliff and the doglions were closing on him, working their way up the slope, their jaws hanging open and slavering. Thousands of feet below – he suddenly could make her out, standing clearly among the cane – was his Khanyi.

She was looking up at him, mouthing something he could not hear and beckoning him to jump – but to jump was to fall and die – but she was somehow standing below him in another landscape on another level and to jump off was to live because the doglions were on him; he could feel their breath behind him. She would catch him. He took a breath and jumped off, flinging himself towards her. He could see her looking up at him even though she was far beneath him, and he awoke with the sudden start that comes with the sensation of falling. A desperate physical convulsion of the body, jerking himself away from the monsters and escaping away from death and towards life. This had woken him.

Never, never before had he experienced such realistic images, or felt a dream so vividly. He was still dazed and confused, and got up and flung open the bedroom door to check behind it for the doglions, then threw back the curtains, still unsure and barely awake, until he came back to his whereabouts and his senses. The lions could not talk, the water was warm, the platform a refuge.

It was dark, raining gently, cold, and the street lights were playing over wet roads outside.

There were no lions, no sharks and no dogs. He was in England in his house. It was 3.20am and the house was silent.

He went in late to work the next day, and asked Emma for a meeting with the boss. They met that afternoon, the first time he'd seen Brian to talk to since leaving to wrap up the estate. It felt like ages had passed. 'Good to see you again, Matt. I've already had positive feedback from the Russians. It seems your repair has been 100% successful again. Well done. How did it go?'

'Well, you know Mr. Pearson, we had the usual snags and a few delays, but I think I got it gas tight. The x-rays showed it was a good repair: no inclusions, no leaks.'

'Good, good, I knew I could count on you. And how about the other trip, your family business, in South Africa was it? That little place with a king chappie. How did that all work out?'

'Well, er, Mr. Pearson, I mean Mr. Brian, that's what I want to see you about.'

'Yes, yes, go on. D'you have to go back, not complete yet, hmm? Takes a devil of a long time these things, never easy, lots of loose ends, don't envy you, laddie.'

He tended to speak in a kind of verbal shorthand.

'No, wrapping up the estate is getting sorted out. It has been slow, but it's going okay. But something else has come up.'

Brian was not a managing director for nothing, and it wasn't the first time he had seen something in a young employee's face, either male or female, that somehow hinted that an affair of the heart had displaced everything else in their life as a priority. His internal radar switched instantly to full power. His voice took on a gentler tone, less businesslike and more personal.

'Well, why don't you tell me about it, Matt. We've got the time.'

He then asked Emma to hold all his calls. This had never happened before and made Matt even more nervous.

'Would you like some coffee, Matt, or a cold drink?'

Matt agreed to tea. He felt like he needed a Scotch. He had intended to run this past someone his own age first, informally, but the chance never came up and now he was having to explain his feelings to his boss, unrehearsed, the last person he wanted to tackle the subject with.

He had written his resignation letter that morning and had it with him, but was already starting to regret it, but he felt at the same time that he owed a proper explanation to Brian, who had always been very fair to him.

'When I was over there I sort of met someone, and I've promised to see her again… and I want to go back and be with her, Mr. Pearson.'

'Aah, I see. Well these things happen, laddie. Are you planning to bring her back over here, Matt?'

Brian's mind was already running desperately over the impact this might have on the business. Matt probably wouldn't be so keen on the long distance overseas trips any more, and the firm would lose the full focus of one of its most valuable staff.

'You met her while you were over there, did you? Local girl, is she?'

'Yes. She used to work for my brother's family but in the time I was there we became sort of involved and I'm sorry to tell you this, but I want to resign and go and live there.'

This really surprised Pearson. It both shocked and upset him. He sat back in his big leather chair to think. They had invested substantial sums of money in Matt's training, knowing that there was always the risk of losing him to the competition, but he hadn't seen this coming. It seemed out of character.

'Well, that's a very big step. She's not, ahem, I mean you haven't, I mean none of my business, private matter and all that, but she's not in any kind of trouble, is she?'

There was an awkward silence.

‘No, it’s nothing like that, Mr. Pearson. I just found that there is quite a demand for the kind of work I do there, and I thought I would go back and try and make a go of it, and make a go of it with her as well.’

He wasn’t explaining himself well.

‘I’m hoping we will get married,’ he added, as though saying this added a layer of security and respectability onto his rather vague plans.

Brian had seen this sort of thing before, and seen it all go horribly wrong. There was that young Rupert chap once whom they had lost in Brazil, to a carnival dancer, much the same story. It had all ended badly.

‘Look, Matt, I’m sure she’s a very special lady but one doesn’t want to rush into these things. It’s a big step. Have you really thought this through? I would guess the opportunities for your skills over there were pretty slim, surely? Tell me a little about her, and a bit about the work opportunities…’

He was careful not to hurt the young man’s feelings. He had often wondered why it was that Matt had stayed single for so long. He suspected there was no shortage of interest from the young ladies in the firm, but despite this he’d remained unattached for as long as he’d worked there. He never even heard about a serious girlfriend through Emma’s far reaching grapevine.

‘Well, Mr. Brian, we became friends at first, and she helped me to sort things out with the estate, and showed me around the area, and then we kind of got involved and she’s waiting for me now. She was very upset over thc loss of the family and we helped each other getting over it. She’s got loads of local contacts, and I want to try and set up a business like the one my brother had over there.’

Brian was still thinking that she would be some young European au-pair or helper based over there and working with the Barton family. Maybe a local farmer’s pretty daughter. Perhaps she was playing the sympathy card, making him feel sorry for her. It was hard to gauge what had happened from a distance.

'Well, I'm happy for you Matt. We all hope to meet the right person one day. What's her background, where is she from? What does she do over there?'

Matt was thrown by this. If he were to answer truthfully, his whole idea would begin to sound a bit daft. But he liked and respected Brian, and wanted to be honest.

'She's a local girl, sir. She has family there, and she speaks the local language. Everyone knows her around there and she was a big help to me.'

He didn't want to call her a maid or domestic worker.

It was all going wrong. As soon as he mentioned the local language, Brian's eyebrows rose a little as though he had worked something out. In a kindly voice he asked, 'What's her name, Matt, this young lady who has stolen your heart away?'

'She's called Khanyisile, but I call her Khanyi. It means light.'

'Oh right, means light does it? That's very pretty, very unusual that is.' He began waving his right hand around in small circles, searching for the words. 'Is she, has she, er, that is to say, does she, I mean where are her parents from?' He wanted to ask something else but couldn't think how to say it.

'Mr. Pearson, she is a Swazi girl. She's not a European girl, not a South African. Her home is there. She meant a lot to my brother's family and now she means a lot to me.'

'And you want to go back to her and make a life out there with her?'

'Yes sir, I do, and I'm sorry but it means I have to tender my resignation.'

Brian tried another angle. 'It seems to have happened very quickly, Matt. Have you got engaged yet or are you both still thinking about it? I mean, you've a solid future here, I hope you know that, and we all value you very highly. I planned on you moving into a management position over the next few years, when you'd had enough of the travelling. I mean, I'm sure she's a lovely person, but you only just met the girl, bit of a different culture and so on. Are you sure this is the best thing for you? Would it not be best to bring her over here for a bit and see how you get on?'

Apart from the loss to the business, he was genuinely concerned for Matt. He hoped the young man hadn't met someone while grief stricken and then been taken advantage of. He had always been a person who hid much of what he was feeling inside. He felt rather guilty. He had been fond of Matt, and was wondering if they had handled the matter of the family loss as well as they should have. Maybe he ought to have arranged counselling for the young man. Emma seemed to think he was handling it okay and she very seldom got things wrong. He was often guided by her in these matters.

Matt thought miserably about Khanyi sitting in his little Northern England house, looking out at the rain, far away from all of her immense family. Away from the sunshine and the dogs. He knew it wouldn't work. He sat back in his chair, feeling a great weight off his shoulders and sighed.

Pearson watched him keenly. 'How are you coping with the loss of your brother, Matt? This must have all been very hard for you, terrible shock. Have you had enough time off for yourself? Is there anything more we can do for you?'

'No, you let me go over there and sort things out, you gave me enough time and I appreciated that. I think we are coming to terms with it now, but it's been very hard.'

'Well, I'm not a person to make people stay who want to leave. If you have thought it through and have really made up your mind, I have no choice but to accept your resignation. But do keep this in mind, lad: if things don't work out and you decide you want to come back, don't hesitate. I'm just a phone call away and there'll always be a place for you here. I mean that. You have been a great asset to us, a great asset.'

He paused, looking out the window to collect his thoughts.

'In fact, if you run into trouble over there, or if there is anything we can do from here, I want you to call. You know we'll always help you, lad.'

'Thank you, Mr. Brian, it's kind of you to say that. I'm sorry about this.'

'Well, these things happen. Good soldiers fall, and they always say you can't stand in the way of love!'

Matt passed the envelope over to his MD who opened it and rapidly read through the carefully worded resignation letter. He had just under a month of Matt's time left, and would have to select the work carefully. It was going to be very difficult to replace Matt Barton, but they would weather the storm as they had done before. He just hoped for Matt's sake that he wasn't making a mistake. He'd certainly miss him.

People like Matt didn't come along very often.

They agreed on the details of his notice period. Brian spoke briefly about sorting out the financial details with payroll and HR, and Matt stood up, shook hands, thanked him and left.

It hadn't been easy for either of them.

Chapter 21

Over the next month, Matt had a mixture of assignments, some easy ones in pleasant places, others harder postings and technically more challenging. He travelled to the north of Spain where he worked in a new refinery processing olive oil, then flew back to the UK and was almost immediately assigned to visit an Indonesian plant that extracted oil from some kind of hard nuts they grew there. It was very hot and difficult there and he didn't enjoy the trip. Back at the firm, there was talk of him going to a place making rum in Barbados, and he was glad when they sent someone else. The days and airports and different jobs were blurring and flying by. He continued to phone Khanyi as he had promised to, every week or so, sometimes at odd times and from odd places.

She had begun knowing it was him calling even before answering the phone, and she sometimes answered breathlessly as if she had run in from outside, or sounded drowsy and sleepy, the strange noise coming through the phone and the delay making her immediately aware it was an overseas call.

'Hello, it's Khanyisile speaking, this is the Barton's house…' hoping it would be Matt.

Her voice made his heart skip a beat every time.

When Khanyi had altered the way she dressed, other things had also changed and become subtly different in her life. She hadn't realised it, but she had suddenly become very attractive and looked young again. Changing her appearance, wearing her new jeans and brighter colours, somehow opened her up to a completely new type of people, to different conversations, quick, light hearted and fun, and it wasn't only proposals of sex from young men that the elders were so determined to prevent. They discouraged single women from even talking to men at all, unless they were already approved, acceptable men, bellowing at the young women that loose talk and listening to flirting was sinful and dangerous, leading to loose morals and inevitable pregnancy. The idea of any innocent friendship was inconceivable and never mentioned.

Off duty, she usually wore a white blouse and blue skirt, never realising how unapproachable and stern it made her look. She looked serious without meaning to, older than she was, and gave off the image of a strictly raised young woman, either on her way to a devout service, or coming from choir practice. It had shielded her from many of the things going on around her, because she never spoke to 'those people' and they in turn seldom spoke to her.

But she began to think that maybe the Umfundisi was wrong, telling her that all these other people were bad. They were fun, the young people she would meet in taxis or on the bus. She liked talking to them and they often made her laugh. They weren't all bad people, just normal people like herself.

She could talk to them and listen to them without giving up any of herself or her beliefs. It was not true that all the men wanted to sleep with her. It was an exciting time for her, because so many things that were normal to other people were new to her.

Calling from Spain one evening, Matt told her his important news. 'Khanyi, I want to tell you something. It's all fixed now. I'm leaving my work here so I can come back again. I resigned from my job a few days back, and my boss has accepted it. I have booked my flight back to South Africa on the fourth and I'm going to see you again soon.'

Khanyi felt herself tingling with excitement again.

'Hau Matt! Hello. Thank you for telling me. I'm very happy if you are coming back again soon. I wish you could come even tomorrow. I would like to see you, but everything is still fine here. There's no problems so far; the dogs are all fine and Ndepethe he says I must greet.'

'Thanks Khanyi, love, and what's the news there? Are you keeping well? How are things going? How about you, how are you doing?'

So many questions at once were confusing to her. She felt her heart jump when he called her 'Khanyi, love.'

She told him that Melanie's father had visited for a few days, and she had explained to him that Mr Barton's brother Matt had visited and was coming back. He had been very kind and asked to take a few small things from his daughter's room.

Matt said that was fine.

She said that many letters had come, that they had no electricity last week, and that the grass cutting machine was still working but short of petrol.

They were excited to hear each other's voices again and he would ask her too many questions at once, or ask complicated questions with double negatives, then she would misunderstand him or begin answering while he was still speaking. She was often confused about where he was in the world and couldn't understand how he kept changing countries without resting. They would sometimes both speak at once and then both stop and wait for the other one while the voice caught up with their thoughts. The long satellite delays disjointed them, and the resulting conversations were often unsatisfying and stilted.

'I am so looking forward to seeing you again, Khanyi.'

'Where are you now, Matt? What is that place, is it nice?'

'How is the weather? Is it getting hot now or is it still like it was when I left?'

'You left that other place?'

'Did you get the card I sent you from Russia, or hasn't it come yet?'

'You mean a card, Matt? What card?'

She was unused to long distance calls, desperate to please him, and he wanted to say so much to her that he ended up saying too much, confusing her.

'Yes, its getting hot but not too much. Matt, when are you coming? I couldn't hear the day.'

'I sent you a card. Did you get it?'

'I got a postcard from you, it came yesterday, from Russia. Where is that place full of snow? Are you still there?

'I'm in Spain, Khanyi, it's nice and warm here.'

'Spain, where is it, is it cold there? It was raining here but it was too little.'

Their efforts to communicate floundered but he always ended their calls trying to make certain that one important message got through.

'Khanyi, can you hear me now? I love you and I'm missing you, and I'll see you soon!'

He waited while his voice bounced off the satellite and carried through the ether. Her voice would grow small and softer.

'Thank you, Matt. I also miss you. I am here waiting for you. Thank you for phoning, Matt, ngiyabonga, stay well.'

She wasn't always sure if she really loved him yet and didn't know how to respond, but she was thrilled by these calls even though they often ended awkwardly. The thought that he was calling from so far just to speak to her was exciting. His accent had grown more noticeable from being back in England, and he spoke too fast for her to easily understand, faster than she was used to.

When she was puzzled her voice sometimes sounded a little flat, subdued and quiet, as if she were sad, and when she knew the call was coming to an end her voice would grow even softer, leaving him wondering if he had upset or left her happier by phoning. Sometimes he hated the phone calls.

For him, just the sound of her voice, their disjointed little conversations and even her accent was like a healing balm washing over his soul. Just hearing her voice answering and responding to him lifted his spirits. It hardly mattered what they said.

He was used to struggling with long distance communications. She was not.

It didn't matter. Even if they kept missing each other's responses, when he heard her voice he could picture her standing by the phone, he could see her listening acutely and could tell when she was smiling. Imagining her there was warm and comforting. He was glad to be kept so busy, because it made time pass quicker.

Matt had decided not to sell his house, but made arrangements with a local agent to let it, fully furnished, once he'd gone. He gave them a mandate to pay his rates and taxes, collect the rent and keep an eye on the place. It was a steady, easy income.

He asked Salikh to arrange to air freight a heavy crate of his belongings out to Swaziland, and started to pack up most of his clothes, a few special tools, some of his favourite music and electronic goods and, although his friend was sad that he was leaving, he got him a very good deal on the freight charges and greatly simplified the whole process.

It was a complicated business and each time he returned home from a work trip there would be a pile of important looking mail lying under the letter box behind his front door. There were more insurance documents concerning his brother, more forms to fill in, customs declarations, UK export documents, air mails from the South African provident funds and life insurance firms, but nothing personal. The airline had finally mailed out a short, tersely-worded form letter, pre-printed with the directors' signatures, expressing their deep condolences and confirming that items of wreckage had been found over a large area of ocean off the horn of Africa, but that no personal effects or human remains had been recovered. There had been a total loss of life, cabin depressurisation would have been instantaneous, the aircraft broke up before hitting the water and did not make a landing and all passengers and crew would have passed away almost instantly and probably at high altitude. The pilot had made a brief mayday call and indicated a total loss of control. The aircraft transmitters gave its last position and there was no evidence to suggest that any technical fault had been responsible for the loss of life. A US dollar payment would be made for every passenger lost in the incident and they required next of kin to submit certified bank details.

He read it with a heavy heart. It seemed a very cold way to describe the loss of Melanie, Patrick and their lovely children, and the end of their young lives. Matt had a few tearful drinks after reading this letter, and deliberately didn't phone Khanyi that evening.

Chapter 22

Brian Pearson had saved Matt's best trip till last, sending him up the motorway to Scotland, to work on some very high grade stainless steel fittings, brass tubes and copper urns, part of an historic distillery that was being rebuilt and refurbished. He put everything of himself into this repair, keen to please Brian and also determined to impress the grim-faced West Coast Scottish brewers, whose grizzled foreman had been less than welcoming at first. The repairs were both involved and complex, with a lot of measuring, difficult fabrication and high quality finishing, because the section of the distillery he was repairing was part of a visitor centre, and it had to look artistic as well as work properly.

He enjoyed the challenge and finished off a stunningly-crafted repair in keeping with the age of the buildings. He even matched the colour of the finished welding to the pipe work. When he had finished and pressure tested everything and the distillery had signed off the work, they presented him with a dusty, ancient wooden box containing an odd-shaped cobwebbed bottle of twenty-five-year-old single malt from their private reserves, a hugely expensive private stock whisky that was never sold on the open market. He decided it was to be his parting gift to Brian Pearson.

Having said his goodbye to the dour Scots brewmaster, and having packed up all his kit, he decided before leaving to go for a little walk around the old, picturesque stone buildings, heavily weathered, covered in lichen and battered by the mighty storms of the North Atlantic. Behind the grey walls on the hillside far above the buildings there was a little brook running out of the peat, from where they drew their pure filtered water, and he walked up close to it, watching the sparkling crystal clear water breaking onto ageless black rocks. The peaceful, timeless splashing noise suddenly took him back to Swaziland. He lay down on the soft, thick grass, looked up at the rushing clouds and thought about the past few weeks.

That trip had been so different. There was so much sunshine. People always greeted each other. Things happened differently. Time seemed to first be available for people exchanging pleasantries, and then was allocated a very distant second place for business.

And there was Khanyisile. Her smile, her walk and the way she looked at him.

He had felt a different pace of life in Swaziland, and a very different approach to things. It took some adjustment. He was tired, and his thoughts drifted away, back to the sunshine, the different pace of life and the cane fields.

On one of his last few mornings there, he had been woken by the clear noise of water splashing on the ground and went out looking for the source of the noise. There was a large water tank near the house, standing on an old concrete platform. It had to be high enough to supply the geyser in the roof, and feed the farmhouse and several other outbuildings in the vicinity. It was filled to overflowing, and clean drinking water was pouring onto the ground. The water splashing was the noise he had heard.

He walked up to the small group of people standing around watching the water falling from a height, greeted them and asked, 'Why is it spilling?'

'Simeon, he never close it,' replied one of the labourers.

'Where is Simeon?'

'Aah, he's to Dvokolwako.'

'Why is he in Dvokolwako?' He had never heard of this place, struggled to pronounce it, but knew it was quite far away.

'He have take a leave to see his father,' another added.

'His father have called him. He is very sick.'

'He is very old, very old, almost late...'

'But when is he coming back from leave?' Matt exclaimed.

'I hope in September,' one of the elders replied, then pointing out the obvious. 'The problem, it's here.' Pointing upwards, they showed him a big brass tap halfway up the tank, next to the galvanized access ladder.

'Why don't you close it?'

'We don't know to. Simeon, he can be angry.'

Another bystander, emboldened by the growing conversation, chipped in, 'Even last time when he's gone for a leave, it's losing too much water for over two weeks.'

The washed stones and worn hollow underneath the overflow showed this to be true.

Matt looked around at the little gathering in some puzzlement.

'Can't we close the tap?'

'We don't know to Simeon.'

'Well, what about if I close it?'

After some discussion, there was tacit approval about this course of action.

'It can be better. It's almost close to full.'

Matt looked at them amazed and almost shouted, incredulously, as the English often do,

'But it's pouring out of the top! It's not close to full, it's completely full!'

'Yes, almost over full,' they all agreed, nodding wisely.

He climbed up the ladder, quickly closed the tap and the water stopped flowing.

There was a silence. Just dripping from the water tank.

'Simeon, he can want to know who is it the one who close the tap,' a voice added in solemn tones of disapproval.

'The tap is for Simeon,' a third added. 'Now we are going to shortage of water.'

'Well, when he comes back in September you can tell him it was me. My name is Matt Barton and I live there at Barton's farm.'

'Okay. We are going to tell him. Thanks about that, Button.'

They pronounced it like a button.

Within a day, all the houses had low water pressure, and by the afternoon it had run out completely and a small delegation stood mournfully at the gate, explaining through Khanyi that they had come to inform him that, owing to his actions which affected the water tank, there was now too less water (the water had run out completely). None of them would turn on the tap.

Matt walked over to the tank, climbed up the ladder and reopened the tap, but not quite fully, hoping that the water coming in might more or less match the volume of water going out.

This startling breakthrough reduced the water supply, and was so successful that he instantly became the unofficial controller of the tap, the umlungu with a magic touch. He never did meet Simeon, and didn't know it then, but anyone wishing to touch the tap in future was always sent to 'Mr. Button' to seek permission first. This included Simeon himself, so it didn't turn out quite the way he had intended.

The daydream ended when a seabird's call roused him, breaking the silence. He smiled, coming back to his chilly Scottish surroundings, thinking about the people he had met and how different life was over there. It had grown very cold now and clouds were gathering over the sea. The sun set early that far north. The west coast of Scotland came back into focus and a bitter wind set the grass and heather waving. Sheets of rain were falling in grey veils out to sea. It was time to go.

His last day at work was an odd mixture of feelings. He was elated because he was going to see Khanyi again in a day or two, but sad because he might never again see the people he had worked with for several years, some of whom he knew well.

He was given a long, fragrant, bosomy, very tight hug and a squeeze by Emma, which surprised him and made him blush, and Brian had laid on a few trays of snacks and drinks for the whole firm. They gave him a little chromed piece of machined steel with an almost impossible welded join mounted on a hardwood plinth, and he made an awkward, very short and clumsy farewell speech.

Some of the younger women kissed him goodbye and cried a little, and Salikh came over and gave him a big hug, his bristly black beard scratching against Matt's neck.

'You look after yourself, mate, and gi'me a call sumwhen. Coom back if ye don't like it out there with them darkies, Matt. We'll be happy to have yer!'

Mr. Pearson said he was really grateful for the rare single malt. The trays of snacks were empty and most of the staff had gone.

It was over.

Chapter 23

THERE WAS REALLY VERY LITTLE to take with him. A few odd remnants of work he had done, some little mementos of different trips. A wooden camel from Dubai, a little brass elephant from somewhere in India, a strangely-shaped stainless steel flask and tap from Russia, engraved in Cyrillic writing, and a photograph album. He had never lived in one place long enough to accumulate much of sentimental value. His house was mostly packed up already.

He left his suitcases in the hallway and went out for a last dinner at a local pub, finding a quiet table near the fireplace and steadily working his way through the heavy north country meal and a pint. He looked about at the dark round tables and soft leather chairs, the old horse brasses, beer taps and beer mats, taking in the oddly familiar smell of old spilt beer, carpets, tobacco and perfume. It was all coming to an end. New beginnings.

Finally, the next morning dawned, and that evening he would fly out of the United Kingdom. Being so used to frequent air travel, he was well organised but found himself spinning in an unexpected whirlpool of mixed emotions. He wanted to see Khanyi again badly, but felt that he was also leaving a lot behind. He just wished he could talk it over with his brother or someone he knew well. Brian Pearson hadn't divulged the reason for him leaving to anyone else or, if he had, they hadn't talked. He suspected that Emma had worked it out already from the way she looked at him, and that special hug, but the only person he had confided in a little bit was Salikh. He had been sympathetic but had sounded a warning.

'It's very different out there in darkie land, Matt, and there's nowt like home. Mek sure you've got the right wench before you go an marry her or you might end up reely regretting it,' were his final words.

He wished it had been a stronger endorsement.

To simplify travelling with big cases, he had booked a taxi to take him right to the airport. The same cab service he often used before duly arrived in the road outside, punctual as always. He didn't want to be alone in the back with his thoughts and found himself climbing into the front of the big saloon and, as they hit the motorway, he began unburdening himself, and explaining everything to the Polish taxi driver, whom he recognised from before.

'I am Janislav Kopec, but is more easy for you to call me Joe.'

He had a short, pointed beard, and always wore the same communist style soft navy blue cap. Joe listened carefully, nodding occasionally or grunting, but driving along in silence as Matt began and took him through everything that had happened.

He found himself explaining about the death of his brother, finding their house, their life there, the business, the country, meeting Khanyi, and deciding that he wanted to change his way of life.

He poured his heart out, telling him how he wanted to see her again, and how different he had found everything there. How people behaved towards one another. How big their families were. Slowly his voice petered out and grew less convincing.

There was a long pause as the car hissed effortlessly along the wet motorway, wipers whip-whapping to and fro across the windscreen, revealing brief glimpses of the wet landscape and traffic.

Kopec cleared his throat then responded after a short silence, affording glimpses of one shiny gold tooth. 'Matt, I think I know you for long time now, maybe four years I carry you in car. We never talk like this. You too busy always, or sleep maybe, because too tired from travel so much.

When I come here to England I am same like you! I have no job,' – he pronounced it ghaff – 'I ghaff no life, I ghaff nothing.

'I leave behind all in this case. My parents, my family, my uncles, my church, my food, house, willage, all gone. But soon after I meet English girl and she decide to become my wife. Her name Eleanor. Now all has changed. She shows me how to live here well. She shows me place to go, she good wife. She ghaff good family. Grandparents for childrens. We ghaff three childrens together, good childrens, nice childrens, clever. Going to good school. Not to be taxi driver like the father.

'This place now ghaff become home for me more than Poland. I like very much to visit sometimes. We drink, we listen music, eat special foods, I enjoy to see family, but I like here, is good place. Why? Because I ghaff found good woman. Woman who ghaff lot of love. Woman who can make me strong in my life. Is enough, is nothing more I need to ghaff. Is simple.'

He laughed. 'Now, when Poland play England football I like for England to win, not Poland!

Is ver' ver' completely different if you ghaff love from good woman. Change all things in this case. She can help you to make life there, new life, good life, can ghaff childrens with you, make family. I think if you ghaff love in your heart, if you feel strong love for that woman, if Indian, Black, even Russian or Japanese, is no matter. You ghaff to go.

'Is simple, nothing more. Is right thing you do now in this case. Go to find woman and keep her.'

It was the most he had ever heard the taxi driver say, and it absolutely answered his question. Matt thought to himself, have I love for this woman? Yes.

Is she a good woman? Yes I know she is.

Do I want to carry on living with her? Yes.

Joe had simplified many things in his mind. The Zen philosophy of a taxi driver spending long hours alone on the road.

Joe had a little more to add. 'All these times I carry you before, you never talk of any woman. Is first time for you to tell me about woman. Is big surprise for me to hear this. So I think you ghaff great love for this woman, otherwise you not tell me. It means she is special lady, perhaps also ghaff great love for you or you never understand one hundred percent clear in your heart you wish to stay there. Now you know. So is simple in this case.'

He sank into a thoughtful silence, concentrating on the heavy traffic and roundabouts as they neared the airport, and cursing softly in fervent Polish as lost travellers cut in front of them, finding themselves in the wrong lane.

Matt smiled and wished there was more time, feeling as though he had tapped into a source of wisdom in Janislav and didn't want the ride to end so soon.

They parked at the drop-off zone and he got his luggage out of the boot. Joe Kopec gave him a quick hug, also a first for them both. His gold tooth glinted in the airport lights. 'Go safely, Matt, is good always to talk. Airport police like to make big trouble for taxis here, I cannot stay long, ghaff to go now in this case.'

Matt settled up, thanked him and tipped him handsomely, then they parted and he walked into the bright business, noise and warmth of the huge terminal without looking back.

It was over.

Janislav Kopec watched the young man's back until he disappeared behind the sliding glass doors, and smiled, thinking of his own new life, and how it had been for him settling in Britain, so many years ago, not knowing anyone in a new country.

He said a short prayer, wished him well and wondered if he would ever see him again.

Chapter 24

In the peaceful lowveld, sitting in the Bartons' still, empty house, Khanyi sat watching the time and wondering if Matt had already started travelling towards her. It was so far. She knew they served food on the aeroplane, and even showed films, so it must be a very long journey. It was hard to imagine where he was and what he was doing.

She knew inside her heart that she had begun to like Matt in a different way, as someone who meant much more than being the younger brother to her boss. The house had become so still after he'd left. She missed him terribly, remembering laughing at his big bowls of cornflakes, his love of tea, gradually understanding the little jokes he made. She had been excited when she heard his voice again. He'd phoned her from many different countries in the time he was away.

When he came, he must show her on the map the different places where he was. Each time they spoke, their conversation seemed to reach a different level from before, raising stronger feelings in her, more intense. Like a new level of being together.

She always hated it when the calls came to an end and she had to ring off. It felt like someone had suddenly taken him away from her and she was left feeling sad and empty. She wondered if she had now changed into an 'in love' somebody, like the people on TV. They always seemed to be kissing and telling people they were in love with them. How did you know when it had happened? Did you look different? Could other people see?

She just missed him so much and wanted him back again.

Everything was different when he was at the house. Time moved so slowly without him and she sometimes felt sick and didn't want to eat without him nearby. Loving is sometimes realising how much you miss that person.

It was a different kind of love that had brought the Dos Santos couple to the Swaziland lowveld. Joao Batista Dos Santos had been sent out to Mozambique as a young man, sent to the almost five-hundred-year-old colony to fulfil his military service. He had started in the service as a diesel mechanic by trade, but after the war had returned to Portugal feeling dissatisfied, awkward in society and no longer able to feel at ease in Europe.

He began drifting into and out of various jobs, psychologically disturbed by what he had seen and done in Africa and hankering after something deep but untarnished. He never settled back there again and started drinking heavily, working for short periods in many different jobs: on construction sites, then for plant hire firms and taking casual building jobs. One day, on a sudden impulse, he responded to an advertisement recruiting workers for Mozambique, and he finally returned to the area where he had fought, living in Mozambique and Southern Tanzania to work on sugar estates. He gradually learned to speak English, fluent Shangaan and some Swahili. He was a hard worker, gifted with his hands, but was always deeply unsettled, and never stayed in one place for long.

One morning he awoke in a cold sweat, shaking and convicted, having had a strong calling the previous night, a vivid spiritual vision that his role on earth was to plant churches. With no theological training and no religious background other than a sudden great hunger, he began devouring the Bible, and soon began to feel empowered to preach on what he had read, always emphasising God's love and humility.

Joao was a bluntly-spoken, strong, immensely practical man, more deeply grounded in the soil and heat of Africa than his ancestral home in Portugal, but he prayerfully and humbly started interpreting the

New Testament scriptures in a way that labourers and field workers could relate to and understand.

He brought colour, a gritty reality and life to the verses, some listeners claiming that they could actually smell the scenes he described, and hear the sounds of ancient Galilee. The people came and listened in large numbers.

He met the woman who was to become his wife along his spiritual journey, one steamingly hot evening during an evangelical revival meeting. He had preached on the beach, standing on the sand in his bare feet under a dirty, white tarpaulin in Beira, facing the Indian Ocean, within earshot of the surf. His face and the villagers and workers listening to him were lit by many paraffin lanterns, all swarming with insects.

She came up and stood at the edge of the gathering and he noticed her, and lost his train of thought completely. He meandered off script and became tongue tied and confused.

Teresinha Da Cunha was a strikingly beautiful woman of complicated and ancient North Indian, Portuguese and African ancestry, with dark glossy hair that fell in ringlets onto her golden brown shoulders, framing a lovely face and emerald green eyes. He was instantly smitten, spoke to her after the service and began pursuing her daily until she eventually agreed to marry him.

Their engagement did not go down well with her family, who had spent a great deal on her foreign education and expected her to meet and marry a doctor, a lawyer, or at least a successful Portuguese business man, not an itinerant pastor, soldier and one-time diesel mechanic. But he adored her absolutely, he would have happily died for her, and could scarcely believe that God had seen fit to allow this stunning young woman into his life.

They were so different looking as a couple. He was broad shouldered, Mediterranean-looking, with warm, humorous, deeply expressive brown eyes – a strongly-built man with a workman's big, rough hands, his face often showing the beginnings of a dark beard –

while she was darker-skinned, tall, fine-featured, almost Ethiopian-looking. An African princess, beautiful and elegant, who had been raised as a Catholic. They made an unlikely but blissfully happy couple, very supportive of each other and deeply devoted. She had never been with a man so utterly committed to his calling, and knew he was passionately in love with her. He hated spending any time away from her.

After spending some years drifting between several Southern African countries, they had ended up in the tiny kingdom. They rented an empty estate house and began a small fellowship of fervent believers in the Swaziland lowveld, where his preaching and her singing and personality began to attract new followers. He would supplement his income by taking on any work he could get, helping out at farm and truck workshops for cash. She was able to find some well-paid translation work for foreign aid agencies working in Mozambique.

Sunday mornings would see an extraordinary mixed gathering of local field workers, wealthy white expatriates, young couples, Afrikaans farmers and their wives and families, senior local management, all manner of tradesmen and people of all ages, from students to pensioners, some travelling great distances to gather and hear Joao Batista speak.

He was humble and straightforward, but his words and messages were abundantly clear and, after Matt left, Khanyi, who had been hearing about this house group, decided to attend. The numbers had already swelled to over a hundred, and could no longer be contained in the small house, so Joao Batista used to stand on a creaking wooden platform under a shady tree and preach to people seated and lying on the grass, like early preachers of a bygone age, to the sound of wild birds and the wind rustling through the trees and standing cane fields.

He delivered short, uncomplicated, grounded and powerful messages that related to daily life, sermons and explanations of the

Gospel that would be repeated verbatim, many times over, to those who were unable to attend.

For Khanyisile, it was like finding water in the dry season. When Matt returned she wanted him to come with her and meet them.

Khanyi found in Teresinha a strong African woman of great beauty, with deep roots in the region, who had successfully melded and forged two different cultures into a partnership, and had already encountered the hostility and difficulties common to many mixed-race marriages.

She was a kind somebody who accepted her for what she was at face value, as a friend and sister. She responded without prejudice, making no judgement about their relationship or her past. Khanyi found it easy to confide in her, and felt that she could ask her for advice on any subject. They gradually became close personal friends, deeply bonded in their nomadic histories and some of the cultural parallels that lay between them.

Khanyi had begun to feel surer of herself and to slowly feel a new sense of her own worth. She had become much more confident, even wearing her jeans to the house church one day. These unseemly changes in her attitude incurred the disapproval and wrath of her old Swazi preacher who felt that she had betrayed them. He was convinced she was becoming a prostitute from all the excited gossip and rumours he heard.

She decided to stop attending his church and began instead to listen to Joao Batista. He never made her, or anyone else, stand up to be disciplined by the elders. He never commented on what any woman was wearing, and they were learning to sing many modern songs which she enjoyed. She grew to look forward to these simple services. Khanyi had been gifted with a fine voice, and soon found herself a key part in a small singing group, harmonizing with Teresinha, accompanied by a few other young musicians.

She had never known such a sense of love and belonging, either at home or in her old spiritual life and, as the dark cloud drifted off her heart, leaving it free and clear, she began to feel loved and admired.

Gradually, the pain and shame she had been made to feel for so much of her young life began to ease and lift off her like a spell of bad weather. She became more secure and comfortable among friends and, sensing she now had Matt's support, she timidly began to value herself again. People complimented her and she began to feel loved and supported, with an inner beauty that glowed brightly from somewhere deep within her, some secret part of her soul kept locked away for years. Her relatives would sometimes comment about how different she looked. Some even thought she was expecting. She often thought about Matt, imagining him sitting in yet another plane, wondering about him.

Chapter 25

MATT SLEPT LIGHTLY AS THEY flew steadily through the clear dark night under vividly bright stars, in an aircraft so big that it seemed motionless, a rock-steady man-made platform, huge and timeless in the sky. He woke occasionally and gazed down through the cold window, quietly fascinated, seeing tiny little lights below, fishing vessels and other ships sailing in the Mediterranean Sea. Later he could just perceive even smaller faint pinpricks of light, far from one another, as they overflew the vast desolation of the Sahara.

He imagined ancient peoples crouching around small cooking fires and lanterns, surrounded by their camels and goats, and sensed them hearing the faint sound of an aircraft passing far overhead, wondering if they could feel him too, or if they ever wondered about the passengers and lives up above in the dark skies.

He thought intently about the last few moments of the Bartons' lives. Did they have time to hug and kiss their children? Did Patrick manage to tell Mel that he loved her one last time? Were they able to hold each other at the very end?

His eyes welled up with tears as he looked out, conscious of the miles of emptiness and cold air below him, thinking of their last minutes of life together as a close-knit, loving family, knowing these were their last moments together, falling terrified through thousands of feet into the freezing dark void. His thoughts were scattered and confused, deeply painful.

The most unthinkable ideas and fears piled up on top of each other, and weighed on him heavily and deeply.

They eventually landed and he passed through the big South African airport in a daze, but then felt his spirits rising as he started seeing familiar landscape beneath the second aircraft. His mood was lifting. After landing, he collected his hire car and set off towards the house, in surroundings that seemed less strange now. There was a different smell in the air, and a different light as the summer approached. Turning onto the dirt road, he wound down the windows, to hear better the sound of the overhead sprayers working their way round and round, splashing noisily onto the dirt roads.

He remembered the way easily and soon found himself at the gate to the homestead. It was closed and, as he unhooked the chain and opened it, all the dogs rushed down the driveway towards the car, but immediately stopped barking when they recognised the person driving it, jostling each other aside to lick his hands. He drove carefully towards the house, and saw her coming slowly out of the shadows.

She was wearing jeans and a light jacket and blouse, a little slimmer than he remembered. Her smile was dazzling and as he got out of the car she broke into a run, and ran into his arms. They stood together in the dying light, both talking at once, kissing, hugging, laughing and asking each other questions.

'How are you? How have you been? How was the journey?'

'I didn't see the car, it's not the same one as before, I wasn't sure if –

'Has it been hot? Are you feeling tired? Do you need food?'

'I missed you. It took so long to come back but I thought about you all the time!'

He gently wiped away tears from her eyes.

Matt suddenly felt he was in the right place. He had his arms around her slender waist, and she was standing close, pressing against him. He would never let her go again. She was a part of this land, and he was becoming a part of her. He thought he could feel his brother's presence around them and felt he might be smiling at them together.

She helped him take out his luggage, and Ndepethe appeared from the gloom leaving a trail of tobacco smoke, greeting the young Mnumzane respectfully and offering to help carry a suitcase. There was rather more luggage this time.

'So you have returned to us,' he said in siSwati. 'We are grateful. It's better you are here.'

Khanyi's young body, in the meantime was simply buzzing with excitement. She felt as if everything in her life were coming together. She had been missing a big part of her and that part had come back. If she'd had any doubts about her feeling for Matt, they had gone the moment she saw him again.

He filled the canyons of her heart.

She was at once breathless, excited, happy, hungry and eager. She didn't want to stop touching him. She felt his hands on her waist, at the top of her jeans, sliding round onto her hips, and found it incredibly exciting knowing he was right there, talking, breathing, just being with her again, making her feel complete. She was shy but wanted to caress his shoulders and waist and pull him tightly against her body.

They went inside together, holding hands, unable to stop touching each other.

As he walked around with her, holding hands through now familiar rooms, even the old farmhouse seemed to welcome him back, absorbing some long-hidden part of him into its stone walls, the bricks and mortar, accepting the love between them as something that was needed to make the house become a home and come to life again.

The air between them was alive with possibilities. He kept drinking her in with his eyes, and she felt him looking and sensed he liked what he saw. If she looked back they would want to touch each other again, as if to check that the other person was real. He even smelt different: faint smells of foreign countries and air travel.

They sat closely together and held hands, and talked for hours. He tried to explain his trip to Russia, what had happened in Scotland, the taxi driver's message to him in the car, and everything he had felt, crammed into five weeks of travelling. And she wanted to tell him all about Joao Batista, about Teresinha, about her trip to town, her decision to leave the old church and all the minutiae of her life in his absence. She wanted him to know about everything that had happened and leave nothing out.

He was suddenly deeply tired, relieved, excited, and most of all happy, just being close to her again, smelling her scent, watching her talk and moving her hands to explain things. He felt protective over her, and he sat back and listened to her voice, watching her mouth, her lips moving over sparkling white teeth and the way her hands and face expressed events. Her nose wrinkled when she sniffed. It fascinated him and he was captivated by her.

After their separation he longed to have her close to him again and persuaded her to move into one of the guest bedrooms. The following night was the last one she spent living apart in her old servants quarters.

Chapter 26

News spread, carried like a virus across the country by the occasional passing trade representative, and by Khanyi's friends who talked excitedly about Matt's return to the region and very soon more repair work started coming in. He realised that he urgently needed to upgrade the equipment he used, and located three specialist suppliers, ordering some very expensive welding machines, different spools of welding wire and three cylinders of special welding gas. He went through all the old, dusty workshop outbuildings and cleaned up whatever could still be used, threw out a large pile of scrap, and then ordered replacements for most of the old hand tools. He went into South Africa and bought a powerful generator, big enough to power a welding machine. He visited Amos again and returned with six fluorescent lights, setting them up in the old buildings so that he could continue to do fine work, even in the evenings or on cloudy days.

Over time he began showing Khanyi how to raise an invoice on the computer, using the stack of Galloway Invoices, how to print one out, and to print receipts. She was a quick learner and enjoyed the feeling of Matt next to her, showing her something new.

A farmer would drive in with equipment and she would assist him, coming out to see whatever needed repairs, and carefully copying down any details she could find in her girlish, rounded handwriting: 'One Agricat Hansa 600 Big ripper' then looking around until she found its serial number. After he had thoroughly inspected it, he would tell her exactly what to write on the job card and how to spell any of the words she wasn't familiar with.

Remove and replace broken centre portion, weld and repair cracks on tine mounting pockets. Replace tines No. 3 and No. 4, rebuild mounting points and linkage, replace and reset all shear points.

He would patiently tell her how to write it out, and she would slowly produce a document on the computer and print it. It wasn't as hard as she'd thought it would be to produce a very business-like document that she could email or fax.

Matt worked out an hourly rate for his time, and would calculate an estimate of the labour and the materials needed. He was usually accurate, having spent so many years calculating in advance what he'd need for a particular job, how long it would take him, and then ordering enough materials to complete it. But the process was laborious and made him think back to his old life.

He had begun to appreciate more acutely just how much Salikh did for them, and how clever he was at predicting in advance what they would need, making sure they never ran short, and overcoming all obstacles, shipping it across the world to wherever they needed it. It was a lot harder doing it all yourself, opening new accounts and hustling the suppliers about late deliveries. Matt would find himself unable to finish something for the lack of some little thing that they never even thought about using up in the UK, but which was in scarce supply where he lived now.

But one successful repair led to another and, through word of mouth among the farmers and talk carried around the local community, his reputation quickly spread and he became known as that umlungu in the lowveld who could fix almost anything. On certain rare occasions, he would reluctantly have to turn work away. Either he didn't have the equipment he needed to finish a successful repair, or he felt the item was too badly damaged to be saved. He preferred to do that rather than sully his unmatched reputation for completing successful, difficult repairs.

Years afterwards, they would both tell different versions of what happened between them to intimate friends. She always claimed he had made the first move, one evening sitting closely together on the couch, but he remembered her pulling the front of his shirt in one hand, standing up and walking backwards down the passage, luring him on with the other hand, one finger beckoning, her eyes sparkling and bright. There was a need they both felt, like teenagers in love with an itch that had to be scratched.

A few days had passed after his return, with the tension increasing between them, and neither wanting to make the first move too obvious. But the strength of physical attraction between them had eventually overwhelmed any resistance.

What was true was that Khanyi was the first through the door, walking backwards with difficulty as they kissed, and that they had undressed each other before reaching the bed. They were both a little shy, but also both keen to satisfy each other, and they shared a long and tiring night together, finding their way to an intimate closeness they were both desperate to feel. He was fascinated by her, bewitched by her body and how she looked, and she was equally amazed to find that she could create so much desire and interest in him just by being beside him naked.

They eventually fell asleep, satiated and relaxed, lying close together. When she awoke the next morning, his arm was around her, and as soon as she moved he pulled her closer, reluctant to let her go. She looked over her shoulder at him and smiled sleepily, aware of a new sensation left inside her from the night before, and wanting to feel it again. He awoke slowly, pulled the covers back and just looked at her, drinking in the view, the lighter skin of her breasts, amazed that someone looking like she did was all his, and had spent the night with him.

Chapter 27

Over time, the kind of machinery and local factory components being brought in started getting bigger and heavier. Most of it could no longer fit under the little workshop roof and they needed a bigger yard area for the big items. Matt had no idea how to find someone to help him build, or even what was needed.

They talked about the lack of sheltered space over dinner and the next day Khanyisile made a few calls and put out the word in the local region. Early the following morning the dogs heralded the arrival of three elderly gentlemen, who arrived on foot at the gate like the three wise men.

They were calm, respectful and dignified.

Matt went out to them.

'Sawubona Mnumzane,' they greeted. 'We are the Sibandzes. This is my small father, this is my brother, we are your builders, now we are coming to make a shelter.'

Six months earlier he would have been confused, but now he took this sudden introduction in his stride and welcomed them in. Then Khanyi helped him to translate what was needed.

They decided on a large area, some of which needed to be cleared of trees and bush and levelled, and two of the men began measuring out the area with a very old, worn, almost blank thirty-metre tape measure, discussing the matter with deep murmuring.

Ndepethe offered assistance as the local expert, and bellowed advice at them from within clouds of smoke.

'What's he telling them, Khanyi?'

'He says that the rain comes from that side, and wind from this side, and in the summer the sun is too strong so they must make the roof and wall to be closed, and the wind is going to make everything wet and dusty inside. He says he has lived here very long, and he has never seen storms coming from that side, towards the mountains, so they must make it open that side.'

'Is he right, Khanyi? Does he know?'

'He knows, Matt. He was working here as a small boy when they started planting trees for this garden. He even made lines for the beds and the drive, when it was still in the bush. He knows this place.'

Matt knew better than to interfere and stayed back, busying himself checking on some steel stock and materials for a new piece of work.

After a time the builders gathered politely at the entrance to the workshops, quietly talking and coughing to themselves in the way people do behind a toilet door with no latch.

'They are ready for you to talk to them now, Matt,' Khanyi told him.

He stepped out into the bright sunshine, blinking in the light after the gloom of the workshop.

'So, gentlemen, what do you think?'

They crouched down and one began taking snuff, the other two gazing into the distance as though this meeting were entirely unexpected.

'So we have seen the place now, Mnumzane Button,' the older one spoke gravely. 'There is much work to be done here.'

Matt looked around, wondering what he should do or say next. Khanyi, sensing the confusion, walked out and joined him, listening but standing a respectful distance away from the older men.

'First we have to chase the snakes, then we must slash, then we must skoffel and clean the area, then we are going to dig for poles, then we are going to put poles,' Sibandze announced.

Matt lowered his head and whispered to Khanyi, 'What is skoffel?'

'I will explain later,' she said. 'We must first listen.'

'We are going to mix concrete then we can put the gum poles in concrete. We will make them to be in a line. Then we are going to make a roof frame with wood, then we are going to cover with roof tiles. We will make fence on that side to stop skellems coming at night.'

They stood nodding in agreement, three ancient sages.

'Then we will close that side a little bit against the rain, and this side make it to be down against the wind.'

Matt looked around trying to visualise what they had described. It was much bigger than he had been imagining. He became worried and asked the spokesman, 'How long will all this take?'

'Aah, it can be very quick, not so very much long,' they replied.

'But somehow it can take a little bit long,' one added, to clarify the matter.

Matt was accustomed to being provided with a rather more distinct time estimate than this and indicated with his hands that he wanted something more.

There was some lengthy deep discussion about the seasons, possible rain, heat, prevailing winds and materials, news of weather in other regions and then the older one looked at the ground and said, 'We will finish this job in less than four weeks if we have materials.'

Khanyi asked him something and there was gentle exchange of views. They spoke to her with different, gentle and slightly feminine voices, as though their normal voices might frighten her off.

'They say they can do this work very nicely. It will be straight but there will be only a small concrete floor, they have no mixer. The poles will be straight, and there will be enough space between them for a big trailer or a lorry to come. It will be high enough. If you can agree they can start next week.'

'But what about the price, Khanyi love? How much will it cost?'

She conveyed this question, raising a wholly new topic which seemed to startle the three men.

'Okay, you mean the cost…' nodded the youngest, a man in his mid-fifties, drawing out the syllables on the 'Oh' and the 'Kay' as if this was a long, massively heavy expression heard for the first time and used rarely.

'We are going to discuss.'

They gazed into the distance, thinking deeply, then all three wandered away, retiring under a tree to discuss further.

Matt had grown to understand that this was a process not to be hurried and carried on with what he had been doing. Khanyi went back inside and carried on with some cooking, singing softly to herself.

After about half an hour of low murmuring, he heard a soft tapping on a door frame and turned to find all three men standing in the gloomy light of the sheds. Shafts of sunlight shone through holes in the rusted, uneven old roof sheets, making a dappled effect on the earthen floor. The air was still enough to see tiny specks of dust floating mote like in the bright light. They scuffed at some small imperfections in the floor. One coughed. One busily cleaned the inside of an ear with a matchstick, then examined the contents of his nose.

Matt waited, fighting against his rising Western impatience and choking down any comment.

'We are going to return tomorrow with a quote,' said Mr. Sibandze.

'Tomorrow we can come back,' added another.

'We cannot see this number as for now. We need to take time to discuss and see how many labourers we will need then we are going to tell you.'

'That's fine,' said Matt. 'I can buy the materials if you tell me what you need, and we can do it together.'

'We can be very happy,' said Sibandze.

As they prepared their meal together that night Matt asked, 'Do you know those guys, Khanyi? Are they alright?'

‘They are some of my real mother’s uncles from Siteki,’ she replied, as though that response entirely answered the question.

‘I know them. One is my small father. They are very famous in building, but they don’t work in town. They say it is too difficult. They like building in the bush because then they can think clearly.’

‘Will they come back with a quote?’

‘They are going to come,’ she said in a tone that effectively closed the subject.

He thought of asking why they couldn’t think clearly in town but could think in the bush, then thought better of it. Matt looked at her, trying to work out the hidden undercurrents of her life and family and very quickly giving it up because she kissed him.

They went to bed on that note.

Shortly after 8.00am the next morning there was a commotion at the gate, and he looked outside, seeing two of the same three men standing there. The dogs were barking half-heartedly, just telling the homestead that there were visitors there, but not total strangers and not a threat. He went down to greet them and let them in.

The older Sibandze dug into his threadbare, earthen brown, smoke-stained woollen greatcoat, worn for formality despite the intense heat, and pulled out a dog-eared rolled up envelope, presenting it to him unsealed, using both hands. Matt opened it and pulled out a folded A4 sheet, with several small pieces of paper all stapled together, covered in a bewildering variety of calculations, all neatly and carefully written in pencil. The A4 sheet employed seven startlingly different fonts and read:

DAVID SIBANDZE AND SONS, BUILDERS.
Make it and Complete 1 (oNE) workshop shelter roof sheets at
BuTTon Farms.
Clear area and flatten all.
Make foundation.
Make wall 5m.

Complete 32 ROOF tiles and make Fenice
Fix ROOF and pellins
Put 36 poles in concrete straight
COST E14264.32
NB Mr Button to supplies avery + each materials.

Completing the document were two signatures, and an X against their three respective names. Attached to this were the smaller working pages, each covered in complicated longhand calculations, all written out neatly in pencil.

These set out the pockets of cement and aggregate required, roof sheets and poles, cutting the creosoted poles and purlins to length, and calculated the working hours for a complicated and varying number of men, even working out how many boxes of roof nails would be needed. It was very thorough, and someone had put a lot of effort and time into the calculations.

Matt looked across at the yard and imagined the area under roof. He knew he would take months to complete what they could do in a few weeks, and somehow felt that he trusted them.

He thought about Khanyi as a little girl, being kindly treated by one of these men and how well she knew people in the community. Deciding suddenly, he smiled and shook hands with them both. 'Ngiyabonga, gentlemen. I am happy to accept your quote.'

They beamed back at him, delighted, but although he offered them tea they explained they had to leave immediately to start arranging and finding labour, and would start work on Monday. He asked how they wanted to be paid and they asked for half in cash, the remainder on completion. They did not have a bank account.

They arrived as promised, a large gang of compact, cheerful, strong men who were at the gate promptly every day before seven, worked swiftly, and only stopped for half an hour at midday to eat bread in great chunks, sideways, swallowing it down with Coke. They worked fast and hard. Matt noticed that one of them would begin a song whenever there was something very heavy and rhythmic to be done, like when they used pick axes digging the foundation holes for the gum poles.

One man would start a labouring song, sung to a very slow cadence, swinging the heavy pick way back over his head, with each stanza ending in that deeply satisfying 'umf' noise of steel digging into soil, and this would trigger the beginning of another verse. Some of them sang a harmony in high voices, as if playing the female part of a virtual choir that was not with them.

After a time the singer would be breathing too heavily to sing and another worker would pick up the tool and continue, almost in the same rhythm. When no one had the breath to sing, the tune would continue but as a repetitive slow whistle or hummed melodiously. Matt sometimes stood watching the men working, awestruck at their strength and deeply engrossed.

Khanyi explained that they were singing about themselves, that the words were very old and talked about rising before dawn in the dark and eating porridge, then walking far, then working in the sun doing a man's work that women and children could not do, and that the soil was hard but they were not frightened of it. Then about together gouging the soil like an elephant's tusk and joining it to themselves. She couldn't explain the last part of the song but said it was very old and mentioned that they were Swazis digging their own soil which was also in their blood and belonged to their king, and bulls would also walk on this soil. She would not explain all of the song but said, 'Ndepethe is the real one who can know this song better. This is deep language. I don't know all the words.'

They covered a large section of the back garden, setting the creosoted, strong-smelling gum poles deep into concrete bases and building a well-made, simple, strong and waterproof shelter that allowed him to store all his equipment out of the rain and sun, and work on bigger pieces in the shade. They cut the fence wires and opened up a new back gate and levelled the ground, removing every shred of vegetation and stamping it hard. They made steady progress every day, with very little wastage. The wall went up quickly.

He noticed how the elder Sibandze would berate any carpenters that broke a purlin or wasted a roofing screw, treating each new purchase of materials with great respect and closely monitoring its use. He kept using a few words that Matt soon recognised: pull, straight and true.

Afterwards, the building completed, the young couple raised the fence around the property, making it higher, and after talking with Khanyisile they decided to buy two more puppies from a local village: lean, greyhound-like animals with long muzzles, one brindle, one brown and tan. They were very quiet most of the time, almost barkless, but very watchful and alert, and incredibly fast over the ground. The other dogs growled and sniffed them over a few times from head to tail, then left them alone. As these pups grew into dogs there were now two packs. The original house dogs who were allowed inside, and stayed close to Khanyisile or Matt all the time and a different, rather more ferocious pack of yard dogs who slept in their kennels during the day, very quietly, but roamed freely around the garden at night. They had occasional arguments, but the security system worked. The dogs from the bush kept to themselves, suspicious and wary of strangers.

The building work was completed, and Matt paid off the balance of his debt. It gave him a much bigger area to work under, and allowed him to move equipment outside, but he began to worry about theft. Passers-by could still see what equipment there was, and he liked being able to leave things where he was working each evening.

They employed a huge, silent man as a security guard. The original night watchman who had worked for the Bartons had absconded some days before their intended return date, leaving Khanyi and the gardener on their own. Their new guard had simply walked up to the house, introduced himself and quietly informed Matt that he had seen that they were starting a workshop business, and there was going to be theft of tools from the local skellems and thieves hiding in the local vleis, shacks and villages, so he had come, as he was going to be their security guard. They would not steal if he was there. He somehow put this across without arrogance or conceit, just with a matter of fact certainty. He explained that people feared him. It was settled before it even started.

He never provided many details, only introducing himself as Knox Mkhize. He was a Zulu, an Inkatha warlord from a small village near Tugela Ferry, a giant of a man in his late forties with old battle scars on his head, chest and arms. He stood well over six feet tall, with huge hands, broad shoulders and a powerful build. He often wore a small red doek tied around one wrist, and sometimes wore an Induna's headdress. He was serious, someone who had fought battles and taken lives, not a man given to small talk or jokes.

The dogs took an instant liking to him and would follow him around faithfully, keeping him company at night and lying close to wherever he sat or made his little fire. He was not scared of them and would talk to them softly in his own language, stroking them and tugging at their ears gently, looking into their eyes, telling them that when thieves came they must be brave and not fearful, explaining that they could see in the dark better than he, so they must warn him of intruders. They would listen attentively, cocking their heads to one side and concentrating deeply, as though receiving some secret and detailed instructions.

Knox was already well-known in the region for apprehending three thieves at once at a nearby garage business, and beating them all severely before calling the local security guards, who arrived to find them tied up in a storeroom, two bleeding profusely and needing medical attention, one silent, bleeding and unconscious. A firearm was lost during this incident and he was widely believed to have kept it.

He said they had tried to escape, but one had insulted his clan and Zulu language, one had attacked him with a cane knife and the other one had been carrying a stolen angle grinder so he'd decided to punish them to assist the law enforcement so they would not forget.

In town, the police might have taken a dim view of this, but down in the bushveld his actions were generally applauded and, when the security van eventually arrived, all three were hauled off to prison.

He began working immediately, roaming the property at night.

Chapter 28

EARLY ONE MORNING, A TRUCK with a crane mounted on the back drove noisily up to the back gate. The visit was not expected. Without delay, and before anyone had walked over to the homestead to greet, the truck turned and began reversing into the yard, and the men on the back started loosening chains holding down a big dirty implement, hooking it up to the boom with chains and dropping the truck sides to begin offloading it.

The dogs were all furiously barking and circling the truck angrily. Matt heard the disturbance and came out of the house quickly, indicating to the truck driver to stop offloading.

Khanyi stood at the kitchen door watching, feeling a sense of unease.

Shortly after the truck arrived, they heard another vehicle at the front gate and coming up the drive saw a blue 4 x 4 bakkie, with oversized wheels and a row of chromed spotlights on the roof and bullbar. A very broad, bulky man jumped down from it and slammed the door loudly. He was stocky and wide shouldered, with a short neck, his skin heavily tanned and freckled, with short spiky hair and a faint moustache. His huge legs ended in elastic-sided ankle boots, with heavy rolled down socks, and he wore a tight fitting, dusty pair of black shorts, and a grubby dirt stained khaki work shirt.

He walked towards Matt, pulling a pack of cigarettes out of his chest pocket. Accompanying him in the front was an enormous, dark muzzled blonde dog, sitting royally in the passenger seat, while two elderly farm labourers sat smoking in the open back, fearful of the pack of farm dogs.

The stranger walked towards Matt, shouting at the Barton's dogs, all now giving voice, to 'Fuck off,' and, 'Voetsak!'

'Ja, morning. Listen here, I heard you people fix these things. I brought this plough for you to fix. Where must I tell my coonboys to offload it?'

Matt was startled by the remark and began to answer coolly. 'I'm Matt, just wait a bit. I need to inspect it before you leave it here.'

'I'm farming near Nhlangano. Hendrik Van Schalkwyk is the name. VS Ranches. I heard you fix shit like this. What you saying? You can't weld it now? It arredy cost me money bringing it here on the blerrie truck,' he said angrily.

He pronounced blerrie truck like one word, and Matt didn't understand him.

'I still have to check it first and look at the problem,' said Matt, clambering up and into the truck bed. The men who had been unloading it respectfully stood back, giving him room. Van Schalwyk clambered up with difficulty and joined him.

'It's fucked here. The blerrie headstock keeps breaking off.'

The yellow-painted headstock, a massive chunk of machined steel that would normally turn over the heavy plough frame, had been broken and repaired so many times that there was little original steel left to work with. The implement was a heavy, five furrow reversible plough in terrible condition, heavily worn, with blunt share points, two bent and badly rusted legs, and with several misaligned plough bodies and most of the shear bolts welded solid.

It had been welded so badly and so many times at the headstock that there were layers and layers of slag and dirt inclusion in the mass of weld and tortured steel. The original part had been rendered virtually scrap metal, with nothing clean or original left to work on.

Matt stood upright thinking quickly to himself. He needed the work, and wanted to build his customer base, but had a sickly sense of unease about this man.

Hendrik was looking over at the house, and he heard him say something under his breath to the labourers, the younger one sniggering behind his hand at some private joke.

'Is that your kaffir girl, there at the house?' said Hendrik, going on without waiting for a reply, 'Yarra, that's a nice looking piece. I suppose you must be banging that thing whenever you want it, out here in the cane. I wouldn't even mind a bit of that myself.' He blew out smoke, sidled up to Matt and looked at him slyly. 'The blacker the berry the sweeter the juice, hey?'

Matt was so shocked, he felt his mouth going dry, and he suddenly felt nauseated, furious and insulted by the man, just wanting him off the property and out of sight. He looked at the visitor coldly and climbed down from the truck. He had turned pale, sickened with anger.

'She is my wife. Excuse me a minute,' he said coldly.

'Oh shit, sorry hey, no offence hey.'

It wasn't true, but in Matt's mind she was going to be his wife, and it meant the same thing.

He had seen Khanyi subtly gesturing to him with her eyes to come back towards her.

He walked, his hands shaking, quickly back across the yard and past the workshop and stepped into the kitchen. She looked at him with liquid eyes and spoke to him softly.

'Be careful of this man, Matt. He won't pay you. He has tried to fix this thing many times, all over, then it always breaks and he refuses to pay. I think he is a bad man, this one.'

She looked at the truck. 'Why is he always looking like that at my body? All the time you looked at that machine he is staring at me, looking at my breasts and legs.'

Van Schalkwyk was accustomed to always getting his way. A poorly-educated farmer of notorious temper, he was known to be a brutal man, and the way he treated his wife, his sons and his workers was widely talked about in that district. Only the family's maid knew of the black and blue bruises on that thin white woman's body, always in places hidden by her clothes. While he was out on the lands, she would sometimes ask the maid to rub linament onto the injuries.

Bruises punched onto the upper arms, bruises from thumping the rib cage. Punching her pale stomach and pinching and hitting her breasts was a common pastime after a bout of brandy drinking. She had reached a point where she believed it was usually her own fault and absorbed the pain without even crying out loud.

Hendrik would drive uncertainly back to the farm, long after dark, very drunk, missing a gear change here and banging a gatepost there, then come roaring into the farmhouse demanding food. If the meat was undercooked, or over cooked, or if the pap too dry or too wet, if the time it took to serve it was too long, or if it was either too hot or too cold the moment he arrived, he would punish someone, usually his wife. The servants and children, having learnt from experience, would quickly make themselves scarce.

He would take a sjambok or his boot to his teenage sons, or kick their cringing dogs at the least provocation, and only the occasional, awkward visit from sleepy and reluctant labour department officials kept him from meting out the same treatment to his workers. VS Ranches was never in the national news, but featured heavily on the underground unofficial news network that Khanyi was tuned into.

Her intuition was running strong, and she was sure she had heard of this man by his reputation. A younger brother of a girlfriend's sister to one of her uncle's friends had helped the maid who worked at the house when she got pregnant. She had told stories of this man who used to beat his wife, and how she sometimes used muti for horses on her body because she could not ask him for money to buy the right medicine for humans.

Her ancestors were almost shouting at her, loudly warning her, don't touch anything belonging to this man, but she couldn't explain it properly to Matt. She took his arm and tried to explain to him what she felt, urgently warning him, 'Matt, he is never going to pay, even if you fix it. He has taken this thing before to many places, even in Manzini, and they all failed to fix it. Don't try to weld it.'

He hesitated only for a moment, looking full into her eyes, feeling the intensity in her words, and then walked back across to the truck and spoke to Hendrik, who was pulling on a cigarette held in his cupped hand between thumb and second finger.

'Look, I'm sorry but I just can't repair this. I'm afraid it's too badly damaged…'

'Ag nee, fok man. What's wrong with you?' Hendrik interrupted. 'It's just a little crack!'

'No, it's not a little crack, it's totally stuffed. There isn't enough left to repair and I can see that many people have tried already. You need a new headstock.'

Van Schalkwyk's close set little grey eyes blazed with hatred and instant rage. He recalled being mercilessly teased at a braai by some of his drinking buddies, all laughing at the state of the same implement after a fourth failed attempt that had cost him dearly.

'Ag, Hendrik man, that blerrie thing is fucked!' they had jeered at him around the braai, 'Jy moet mos kak and betaal, ouboet.'

He glared at Matt with loathing, convincing himself that he was only refusing to fix it because of what he had said about the sexy looking kaffir woman. He turned and stomped off, swearing and kicking at the dogs, climbed into his 4x4 bakkie, slammed the door and roared off in a cloud of dust, spinning the wheels. The men left sitting on the truck lifted up the drop sides and locked them, tied down the broken plough again and slowly manouvered the truck out of the yard, back to their misery and out of their lives.

Two of them waved, and one had bashfully apologised to Khanyisile and Matt.

Khanyi felt the thrill of knowing that she had saved her partner from a big problem, convinced that she had been guided away from it by those who have already passed.

Chapter 29

THE CALL CAME EARLY ONE Saturday morning, and Matt got up to answer it, rising with shaky legs from a long and delicious bout of lovemaking, the couple's favourite way to start a weekend. The heavily accented brogue at the other end of the line was strong and clear, and carried something of the cold, salt laden, North Atlantic winds and lush greenery of the West coast of Ireland, incongruous when heard among the cane fields of the Eastern lowveld.

'It's Padraic O'Connor calling, I'm down here on the farm near Sidvokodvo, Shamrock Farms. You've perhaps heard of us here? Sure, we've a whole world of trouble here just now. Would you be able to help us at all?'

Matt tried to recall what he had heard of Shamrock Farms, and asked him what had happened, the memory of Khanyi's warm, fragrant, inviting, brown body rapidly receding from his mind.

'Phwell, d'you know,' Padraic replied, 'the lads have gone and broken the fockin' harvester so they have. Sure if they didn't catch the left coulter set hard against a tree stump, and broke the whole of it right in two. It's a fockin' disaster I've on my hands now d'you know...'

They had just started the season and had begun lifting the third of several huge fields of good soil, all sown with potatoes, and the crop was lying in the ground with the foliage bent over and dry, ready to be lifted, acres and acres of perfect potatoes, but without his four row harvester running there was no way he could bring them in fast enough to move to market. The machine was so big it had been assembled on site and, short of stripping it completely, couldn't be moved along a public road.

He explained the situation, needing Matt to come and repair it at the farm.

'Can you maybe try and explain to me exactly what's broken on it?' asked Matt.

'Phwell, the harvest team lads were leaving one of the fields with Simon on the big tractor, but it was almost dark, so it was, and sure he snagged it on one side. The poor boy, he's normally very careful, d'you know? He's the only one that drives it, but it's all bent away to buggery. It's torn the steel frame right at the mounting and pulled the half of itself right back.'

He sighed heavily. 'In the name of all the saints above it's a bloody mess, so it is Matthew! The tractor lads and I tried to straighten it a little with a chain and a ratchet, but all the sprocket alignments are gone now and the focking chains keep flying off and away into the field, d'you know? Now the shakers and separator chains are all tangled up themselves altogether, and it's well focked, and I've not a clue how to weld at all myself.'

There was a pause while Matt gathered his thoughts. 'Have you got three phase electricity there?' he asked, thinking about the damage Paidric was describing, and trying to imagine the machine. He had once seen a beet harvester working in a field in Norfolk, but that was the closest he'd come to anything like it.

'Yes, indeed we do. We've brought it down to the pack shed, and Jeesus there's enough power there, so there is.'

'Mr. O'Connor, could you perhaps send me some pictures by email, especially showing right where its broken, and maybe some from further back, showing the other side that isn't damaged, then I'll know better what to bring. I can get down to you later this afternoon, but I might need to spend the night there. Would you be able to put us up somewhere? I can't make any promises about the repair before seeing it, but I'll give it a try.'

He nearly added, 'So I will,' but managed to stop himself in time.

'Oh Jeesus and all the saints, that's a blessing. I've got a guest cottage on the property. You'll be fine staying there, it's alright, d'you know? I've had our priest himself there before. But I've no clue how to do that at all phwat you said with all them E pictures, so I can't be sending you anything like that. But sure, my young daughter Kaitleen's here, so she is, and she knows all about those things. She's always sending her mother all kinds of pictures from the school, d'you know, so I'll be after asking her to do it right away. Let me call her so she can write down that special computer address of yours.'

Before he could stop him, Padraig O'Connor had dropped the phone noisily and was bellowing in the background, calling to Kaitleen. 'Will you hurry yourself up child, and come now and talk to the man about that electric intermail web address thing. But will you hurry now, because he's after needing some pictures of it so he is. Jeesus Christ.'

'I'm coming, Daddy. I was just finding a pen!'

Kaitleen sounded about fifteen. She knew all about email, and quickly understood what Matt needed. The young girl's voice had an accent much like her father's, but a little less strong, and with a slight South African twang, and she told Matt she would use her cellphone, take the pictures and get them off to him 'just now'.

She gave him her cell number in case it didn't work, and told him her email address, explaining that she might have to send them one by one if they were big files because the line speed was a bit slow on the farm.

She said her father never used the email at all and didn't trust it. He could hear her smiling as she explained. He believed that foreign devils would come and steal all his money through the wires and computers. Matt smiled at the familiar accent, and the casual extent of her youthful competence and computer knowhow compared to her father. He cut off the call, and went back to the bedroom. Khanyi was already up and showering. He talked to her through the glass, enjoying the spectacular view as water and white soap suds slid down her naked body.

'I've got to go to Sidvokodvo, Khanyi, and I might need to stay the night there. There's a farmer down there in trouble with a machine.'

'Do you need me to come too?'

He thought about it, but it would be a boring time for her while he worked, and they needed someone at the homestead with the animals, so they agreed she would stay behind. Khanyi would wait for the emails to come through, and print off some pictures while he washed and got ready.

He asked her to get a message to his assistant to come in to work, although it was Saturday, and help him load the heavy equipment onto the van, and then come with him, packed and ready for a night away. He was a pleasant, hard-working young man, employed to help Matt and learn some of the techniques he used. Musa was a Khumalo, and he had come recommended, having had some previous experience in a machine shop and with a feeling for metal working and a technical college background. He was distantly related to one of the leading Nkomati cooperative farming families. He was a hard worker, was learning to drive and had picked up new techniques fast, rapidly becoming a useful asset to the little business as it grew. Often now, the components brought to them were simply too heavy for Matt to handle alone, and the young man lent his strength to this, while also preparing the steel for the main repairs.

Kaitleen O'Connor was as good as her word, and after about half an hour they were able to print off several clear pictures from her email. She had got his email 'special address' down alright.

They looked through the pictures together over their quick breakfast.

It was a real mess. The mounting turret was broken, with metal torn from metal. The crop lifting coulter had moved sideways and he could see a badly bent frame, and many complicated chains and sprockets, now all misaligned. He could see what Padraic had tried to do, but he had actually made it worse. The whole thing needed to be first chained down and strongly secured, then be straightened and tacked in place, and then welded up again permanently, with additional gussets on the high stress sections and joints. But getting everything straight again would be a huge struggle.

It had a wide, long separator table, and many of the shaker rods were bent. But it reminded him somehow of similar repairs he had done in factories and plants in other countries, often working with frozen steel in cold dark places, or working where it was very hot and cramped, and where the materials were difficult alloys, far less forgiving than mild steel, and there was an even greater time constraint.

He thought he would manage it.

From reviewing the photographs he understood a bit more clearly what he needed to take with him, and began assembling a big load, not only filling up the bakkie, but loading a small trailer too. They loaded the big Lincoln welder, an inverter, cutting tools, angle grinders, some high grade steel stock, various bits and pieces, a hydraulic chassis straightening set with chains, an assortment of trestles and blocks, and a host of other welding materials. The workshop looked quite empty after everything was loaded up and secured.

'Khanyi love, phone him and tell him I'm on my way.'

They kissed goodbye and, with Musa beside him, he drove off in the heavily loaded vehicle, the dogs seeing them off noisily to the gate. Musa had his entire overnight luggage packed in one small plastic shopping bag.

They couldn't travel very fast with the heavy load on the rough roads, and only reached the farm in the early afternoon. The shadows were already lengthening in the dusty yard as they drove up and parked. Padraic O'Connor came out to greet them, a short, energetic, wiry man, with dark eyebrows, shadowed constantly by a pretty little bright eyed Jack Russel terrier, who watched his every word and move as if she understood him.

'Jeesus, you must be tired, Barton. will you be after coming in for some tea before you start at all?'

Matt thanked him but declined, explaining that he wanted to get a good look at things while there was still some daylight. They set off for the pack shed, following O'Connor and his daughter in their old land rover.

The harvester was a very big machine, called a Spudnik, and still quite new. It had done one season and was his pride and joy. Surrounding the pack shed yard were several large trees, and a concrete loading ramp with two steel eyes set in the side, and Matt thought he could use them to chain it up while they tried to straighten it, but the harvester was quite badly damaged. Suddenly a strange and distinct sense of dejavu swept over him. He really wanted to look about him for lions, but saw Musa watching him with an odd, slightly puzzled expression. The boss was acting strangely.

He suddenly felt intensely that he had seen this platform before. It didn't frighten him, but it chilled his soul and he felt himself sinking into it. The steel eyes were just as he remembered . It had concrete sides, and rose sharply, but was surrounded only by neatly graded gravel, tidy parking lots marked with half buried white painted tyres, low flower beds, and trees. The view from the top was just that, a view from the top of a loading platform over the well tended yard and pack shed frontal. He shivered for a moment, thinking about the nightmare lions and the jump he had made in his dream, even peering over the edge to the ground. It was only about four feet high, with thick grass and blackjacks growing in the backfill, and Shamrock Farms was spread all around it. He could see the farmhouse in the distance. No sea water or sharks.

He walked a little way down the slope to lessen the height, and then purposefully jumped off it and onto the ground, the solid thud of his work boots hitting the earth and jarring his knees, a pleasant reminder of reality around him. Khanyi was waiting safe at the house. Musa was with him. No lions anywhere.

They began offloading the tools they had brought, and he asked if it was safe to leave everything there overnight. O'Connor said he only had good people on the farm, and was sure it would be fine, but would have a guard watching over everything all night, and would release his big dogs in the area. He had three Irish wolfhounds, and used them as guard dogs.

They began working together, Musa and Matt helping each other to lift off the heavier components, initially loosening and removing everything that was in the way of the section that needed repairs, and laying the pieces carefully down in order. Padraic watched them for a while, asked if they needed another hand, and checked if they would need anything further and then excused himself, saying he was needed back at the house.

Kaitleen remained behind, a sweet faced, lightly freckled teenage girl with the deepest sky blue eyes, long dark eyelashes, and wavy auburn hair tied in a bushy pony tail. Her skin was as fresh and white as milk. She chatted to the men while they worked, occasionally fetching and holding things for them, telling them about her boarding school, her teachers, her homework, her favourite subjects, her horse, and how she loved coming back to the farm during the holidays.

Matt was working hard. He mostly grunted and asked her short questions, but she chatted away cheerfully, and he found out that her mum was very ill and bedridden, and whenever she was home she would try to cook meals for her dad, the way her mum used to make them. He was originally from Galway. Her mum was a white Swazi. The girl's name was pronounced like Kathleen, but spelt Kaitleen because it was Gaelic. She was one of five children, all girls, and all older than her, but they had moved away, two of them to Australia. Matt liked her. She was not flirtatious at all, very respectful to Musa, just friendly and excited by the unexpected visitors and genuinely interested in how they were going to fix the machine.

She made them laugh when she said her dad had used some words she'd never heard him use before after the driver told him what had happened, and that the bottle of Bushmills had taken some terrible punishment later that night, while he roared to her and the dogs about the heathens living in the land all about them, breaking up the tools of work of an honest farmer.

As the light started to fade, she said she would have to go and begin cooking, and asked if they would need anything more. Matt asked if there were any big lights they could borrow, and she said she would ask her dad, then walked off back towards the farmhouse in the dusk. She was charming and young and it was sweet and refreshing to talk to her.

As it was just beginning to get too dark to see enough to carry on working, Padraic rattled up in the old Land Rover, and began offloading a small generator, some long cables and two powerful floodlights on telescopic poles. He said he'd bought them for doing crop transfers when they used to do night harvesting but they had long stopped using them, and he hoped they would still work.

He muttered to himself and set about fussing over the generator, cursing its little Japanese heart fondly, and reminding it of all its previous wrongdoings, but quickly got it started, then plugged in the two lights. They were immensely bright and before they had even finished positioning them close to the broken machine they had become the centre of attention for thousands of insects that seemed to come out of nowhere in the dark night. Big moths and idiotic fat, buzzing rose beetles, flying around frantically and crashing into the lenses, frying and dying by the hundred.

Matt thanked him and, working under the floodlights, they carried on as the stars came out and chilled as the dew began to settle. The insects with their scratchy little feet would often find their way under their collars and into their shirts, to be removed and flung on the floor.

At 7.30pm, Padraic returned and told them they ought to stop working now, adding, 'Save your strength, lads. Save it for the morning, will ye? You'll be after needing it, so you will, Jeesus Christ!'

He said he would have some food prepared for them and invited them to the guest house to wash up and have something to eat. Both men were very weary by then, after the long drive and afternoon working, and they were glad to stop. Matt's hands were tired and sore, and his body ached.

He was used to things arriving at the workshop already stripped and ready for welding, and had forgotten how tiring it could be, working with hand tools on big, heavy equipment with very tight bolts and nuts. Musa was yawning and said he was hungry and ready for sleep. He was a man of few words, and this, for him, was a lengthy sentence. They expected at best some very basic accommodation and simple food.

Padraic guided them both to a modern, clean little cottage on the edge of his property, and told them 'a little supper' would be coming in a short while. They should make themselves at home and rest. He'd send down a few beers, so he would.

Just as they sat down, both freshly showered, clean, smelling of soap and changed into fresh clothes, a little delegation of three women arrived, each carrying trays laden with food. O'Connor obviously believed that working men needed proper nourishment and had sent them a large bowl of rich lamb stew, crocks of steamed and roast potatoes, mounds of carrots, butternut, sweet potatoes, steamed cabbage and other vegetables, and a heavy treacle dessert with custard. Matt had never seen so much food for two people, and thought back to the days of his standard fare: toasted cheese and tomato sandwiches.

Kaitleen managed the entire operation very efficiently, directing the young ladies in fluent SiSwati, where to put the trays and how to set the table. It was a slick, well-practised process. The table was laid, drinks were set out and, to his embarrassment, one of the women was told to stay behind, just to clear away after each course. They ate heavily and eventually sat back, full and tired, and both went off to their bedrooms.

Musa immediately fell asleep while everything was discretely carried away, back to the main house. Matt spoke to Khanyi on his cellphone for a few moments. She said everything was fine at home, and then he too slept.

The next morning, Matt woke from such a deep sleep that he wondered for a brief moment where he was. Then he looked outside and remembered. The sun was just climbing over the trees and lighting up the quiet garden. At seven on the dot, the same team arrived and with quiet efficiency set about serving them a full cooked breakfast, as though the two men might have starved away entirely during the night.

Kaitleen enquired if they had slept well, and Matt smiled, thinking of how he'd had to uncover several layers of blankets wrapped tightly around Musa's head, and shake him repeatedly to get him to wake up at all. He didn't just fall asleep; he became comatose.

They went straight back to work, and as they arrived at the pack shed they saw the guard walking off in his light brown trench coat, trailed by three immensely big, fierce-looking, shaggy brindle dogs, each wearing thick leather collars studded around with short metal studs. They were quiet, dignified dogs, and walked alongside the night watchman, almost chest high, waving their long curved tails, looking rather like three thin, hairy horses. Musa was terrified of them and asked what kind of animals they were.

Their hands touched the cool metal again, wiping off the heavy dew that had covered their tools and the components. O'Connor had said they would be leaving for Mass shortly, but he would instruct a tractor driver to help move the machine to where they could chain it up. After this was done, Matt chained it into place against the steel rings and began slowly forcing it back into shape. It was a slow process. He had to bend and pull things beyond where he wanted them to be, because he knew they would spring back a little when he removed the tension, and it took a lot of thought, ensuring that they didn't create more damage, trying to repair what had already been bent or broken. He couldn't remove all the kinks, but got it straightened out enough.

By mid-morning he felt ready to start welding, and tacked the main parts of the machine back into place. Then he began welding properly, long, perfect, deep, metallic works of art, while Musa was cutting up small gussets and patches for him, measuring carefully and exactly where each piece was to go and cutting the steel plate to size with a cutting torch, then grinding the edges to a bevel and tacking them in place.

Drawing on his skills and a lot of experience, Matt worked very carefully and slowly fabricated the repair with the new patches, building strength back into the damaged area, and he was pleased to see that they had got the sprockets and chains lined up again. He wasn't going to worry about painting it this time, and while the repairs were still cooling they began gradually reassembling everything they had removed the previous day.

It went back together rather faster than they had taken it apart, now that it was all straight again and, although Padraic, back from Mass, had invited them for lunch, they declined this, preferring to work through and still feeling well fed from the previous meals.

By the middle of that afternoon, Matt finally asked the tractor driver to connect up the hydraulics and try the machine, and it started and ran smoothly and without vibration. None of the chains jumped off their sprockets. He ground off and cleaned up a few of the welded areas, applied some primer where he could, then they began assembling their kit and repacking all the tools on their vehicles.

Kaitleen and her father had come and visited a few times during the day, and had sent down drinks, snacks and tea and, as he lifted the last toolbox onto the van, he saw three large pockets of flawless, creamy Shamrock Farms potatoes and two pockets of perfect oranges neatly laid on the front seats. Padraic never once mentioned the cost, and when Matt got home and invoiced him later that week, he paid the large bill without complaint, even phoning him to thank him and to tell him that the harvester was still working perfectly. O'Connor soon became their unofficial marketing agent in the area, opening them up to many new businesses.

He knew immediately when it was Padraic O'Connor calling, because he would always start by asking, 'Is that yourself, Matthew? Sure now, it's Padraic calling from Shamrock Farms, d'you know?' As though it could possibly be anyone else.

Chapter 30

THERE HAD BEEN A FEW strange, unsettled days of grey sullen skies, high, fast-moving clouds, distant veils of falling rain, visible but remaining in the distance, and the occasional sound of far distant thunder from the deep south of the Kingdom.

An unquiet presence was in the air itself, and time had hung heavy on their hands, the afternoon oddly uneasy. Khanyi, on that day, had been different, irritable and easily upset, and for once even Matt had seemed to be unusually distant from her, wrapped up in his own world and strangely quiet.

She vaguely sensed a deep foreboding, something wicked and dark, and memories flooded back into her mind that she had always tried to forget. She had suddenly and unexpectedly been reminded of the ominous day she had seen the owl, and little signs and trivial things that went wrong kept bringing to the surface painful thoughts of those terrible few days. She wanted to talk to Matt but couldn't properly explain what she was feeling in words. She felt scared for him. It was as though someone was trying to call out and tell her something, but was far away, just too far away for her to hear the message clearly.

She had been on edge during the day and it made her drop a glass, a sharp breakage that upset her more than usual and made her question herself and feel clumsy. Such days were rare between them, and she didn't know how to respond to her misgivings. She thought a lot about her grandmother and mother, wondering if they could feel her inexplicable sense of sadness.

The disturbance, when it came, was loud, the noise intense and demanding. Their dogs just would not stop barking around the back gate. She had never heard them sounding so insistent and ferocious.

Matt went out into the low afternoon light to find out what all the noise was about, shouting at the dogs to shut up, but the unexpected visitors stood around and smirked, and nothing he could say or do would calm the animals down. The animals, sensing a threat, had taken a violent dislike to the three men from the moment they scented them, at that stage still a long way off, moving suspiciously, keeping to the shadows and now lurking around the back gate, never fully in view. The pack milled around, snarling, growling and barking constantly, bouncing on their back legs, banging their paws against the fence and gate and baying to be released.

One of them was baiting the animals, lunging at the fence then backing away, calling the dogs forward and then saying, 'Voetsak!' laughing and pretending to throw stones at them.

There were three of them, youngish men in their thirties, shuffling around in worn, dirty takkies in the dusty emptiness of a Sunday afternoon. He could smell them clearly. They were lean, dirty and all carried the same dull expression of hunger. They smelt of wood smoke, mixed with their own pungent body odours, unwashed clothes and dirty feet. In their clothes, on their fingers and in their hair they all carried with them the distinctive smell of dagga.

One stood smoking, nearest the gate, pulling on his cigarette with sunken cheeks. Their skin was grey and dusty, two had uncombed hair, in short stumpy dreads, the third wore a small red sun hat, perched jauntily over one side of his shaven skull and almost covering one eye. They looked raw and wary, like a wolf pack watching for the right opportunity. Dirty, dangerous and feral, their reddened eyes without emotion, dulled with tiredness and hunger, a deep hostility and contempt coming from the depths of black pupils that had witnessed and taken part in acts of unbelievable violence.

They had been watching the Bartons' place for a while, and timed their visit to coincide with there being no staff on the farm, expecting an easy entrance.

They had been on the run for nearly three weeks, living rough, lying up in the bush with little to eat and little shelter. They had not washed properly or rested in safety in several days, always on the move like a pack of sharks. The gang had run into trouble during a failed farm invasion and assault near Piet Retief. There, the local farmwatch had responded much faster than they'd ever thought possible, arriving in numbers in their fast pick-up trucks, and opening fire accurately and without any hesitation, using shotguns, handguns and high velocity hunting rifles, showing every intention to kill. The farmers had immediately mustered ten different guns between them, attacked the gang and fought back hard, and the three men had fled on foot, escaping through a hole cut in the fence, leaving an elderly Boer couple beaten and shocked but still alive, after failing to break into a gun safe.

The shorter one of the three had been slightly injured by buckshot, and the planned robbery had had to be abandoned. Then, just as they retreated into the dusk, the SA Police had arrived and released sniffer dogs to track them.

These dogs, together with farm security teams on horseback, had tracked and chased them far into the bush and over the border, losing them eventually in the deep remote valleys and rough terrain of the vast, dark, cold Usuthu forests of western Swaziland.

Crossing the border using old dagga smuggling paths, they had jogged and walked for several days, changing directions often, following little known footpaths and game trails through the bush and always keeping well away from roads. Starving, they had headed down into the warmth of the lowveld and some respite, forcing their way aggressively into terrified rural homesteads and small trading stores, kicking down doors, demanding food and somewhere to stay, looting huts and occasionally raping and beating as they went, but they now needed hard cash to bribe soldiers and pay off guides.

They planned to cross over the border into Mozambique using old car stealing routes, climbing up and along old tracks and through secret gaps in the Lebombo mountain range, wanting to rest up in the bush and disappear completely for a while, somewhere the police would not follow them.

Two were locals. The third, taller one, and their apparent leader, was a Mozambican Shangaan, a suspect already wanted in Magude for car theft, suspected rape and murder, and on the run in South Africa.

Matt approached them warily, feeling uneasy and uncomfortable about their appearance. They acknowledged him with a cold smile that did not touch their eyes but did not greet him, the youngest looking one barely rising from a crouch.

'We want food,' demanded the man nearest the gate. 'We must get food. We are shortage of food, we are hungry. We know you have food. We need it, you must give us.'

'Money also, and food. We are very hungry,' added a second whining voice from the gathering darkness.

Matt thought they would not come into the yard with the dogs barking, and affected by the mention of hunger felt they might leave if he gave them something to eat. 'Let me see what I can find,' he said, turning his back on them as he began walking towards the house. He called some of the younger dogs, who would obey, and they reluctantly left the three men at the fence and followed behind him.

He was about half way between the fence and the back door when he heard footsteps running quickly behind him over the stamped dirt yard. He turned and saw one of the men rushing towards him, a gleaming blade held point down in his right hand. The dogs went crazy, racing towards the intruder, while the other two began beating off the animals who had attacked them the moment they'd opened the back gate, swinging at them wildly with a metal bar and a cane knife. They had skilfully managed to trap some dogs on the wrong side of the fence line.

He was startled by the speed of the invasion and had just enough time to scream loudly, 'Khanyi! Lock the door!' but they were very fast and had the element of surprise. The dogs didn't understand what was happening and had split up, some staying with him, some around the fence line and the smaller ones running for the house. He saw one of the men running quickly along and down the side of the fenced area, heading for the back door. One of them hacked at the biggest female viciously on her shoulder, and kicked at two others. They yelped and backed away, still barking wildly.

Matt raised his arm to fend off the knife, making for the workshops to try and lead them away from the house, hoping desperately to find something to use for defence. Running, panicking and looking over his shoulder, he tripped and lost his footing just as the first intruder attacked, swinging his blade downwards, overhand. As he tripped and fell, the intended deep stabbing wound missed its aim and didn't penetrate fully, instead making a deep, agonising wound in the muscles of his shoulder.

He turned round, bare handed, shielding his face and bracing for more pain, facing the man directly and still scrambling around desperately behind him for a weapon, anything he could find to defend himself, all the while watching the sinuous movements of the knife in the gloom. He braced himself for the coming thrust, unarmed and unready.

There was a sudden odd sound, like a blunt axe splitting soft wood, and a soft grunt, and the invader's eyes looked strangely sideways and upwards. Then he dropped slowly onto his knees, wearing a look of numb, confused surprise, turning in slow motion to dully take in what had become of his senses.

Knox, looming tall behind him, then caught him again with a second, fearsomely powerful swinging blow, striking the side of the head again with his ironwood knobkerrie, the sharp knuckled head eating deeply into the soft part of the man's skull, just above the ear. Knife still in hand, the thug dropped and fell onto the dust, lying on his side. His legs twitched a few times and the dogs seized them, worrying them like a terrier shaking a venomous snake. Blood began leaking fast from his head and ear into the sand.

'How many are they, Boss?' said Knox calmly. 'Where are the others?'

'Three, there are three, Knox, but one has got in the house and Khanyi's in there!'

Knox turned and ran straight for the back door, kicking it open, several loyal dogs following close behind, excited now, their blood hot for the kill.

Matt tried to reach up behind to feel where he had been stabbed, and how much blood there was when he heard her screams coming from the house. Adrenalin took over and he grabbed the nearest thing he could, a garden fork, and ran towards the noise. Khanyi meant everything to him.

As he rushed through into the kitchen one of the thieves came running towards the broken back door and he lunged at him with the fork. The man scrabbled under his shirt, and Matt saw the butt of a firearm stuck in his jeans. He had just got it out and clear, and had levelled it at him and was pulling back the slide, when Knox collided with him, pushing him hard towards the fork prongs. He screamed and fired but the shot went high, ricocheting off the tiled wall. Before he could fire again he took a savage blow to the top of his head that felled him instantly.

Knox quickly grabbed the automatic, broke his wrist and disarmed him, then removed the clip from the firearm and pocketed both.

'Khanyi's okay, boss, what about the other one?'

Then, 'Are you okay?'

Matt nodded and turned and they both ran outside, unsure of where the last gang member was. He could feel warm blood running down between his shirt and his back and gathering above his waist.

There was a huge commotion near the back gate again. The dogs had done their work well and had by now cornered the third criminal against the corner fences. He was lashing out at them with a cane knife, and kicking at their muzzles, but they were used to dealing with dangerous snakes and rats and were too fast for him, the one grabbing his arm tightly in its massive jaws, while another grabbed his leg just above the knee, biting deeply into his thigh. The two bush dogs were now in the hunt, leaping up at his face and chest and snapping at him. Whichever way he moved, a set of jaws would find a new tighter grip on his clothing and flesh, teeth tearing, biting and pulling at his legs, his crotch, and at both arms. All the uninjured dogs were now on him, or circling in wait. He was shouting now, pleading, and began screaming at Matt and Knox to call them off.

'Bamba tinjatakho, Hau bamba! eyaluma! Please, the dogs can kill me!'

Knox watched him for some seconds without emotion, standing calm amidst the storm. Then, after gently pushing aside the dogs, he struck him a single heavy blow with his right fist, just under his right eye. It was perfectly timed. The intruder's eyes glazed over and he fell to the ground, releasing the bloodied cane knife.

Apart from the growling of the dogs, still tugging on clothes, biting and tearing at anything they could grip and hold onto, there was a sudden lull.

Matt ran for the house, meeting Khanyi just coming outside, wide eyed and breathing quickly. She was okay, unhurt but still shaking. She had been changing into her night clothes and her nightie was torn. She hugged him and he winced from the wound in his shoulder. She told him that when he shouted she had run into a bedroom and was locking it, but the one moving the fastest had got inside, following her and was just forcing open the bedroom door, unaware that Knox had come in just behind him. Knox swung at him but missed, his heavy 'kerrie snagging the wall. Then, as the man turned and realised his size, he ran, evading capture, but running into Matt with the fork.

Khanyi raised Matt's shirt, and looked at the stab wound and it somehow calmed her. There were things to do. She went immediately into the house for warm water, medicine and dressings.

Knox was relaxed and completely unhurt, casually standing on the back of the man near the gate, still being mauled by the dogs, calmly wrapping a piece of rope around his wrists, as if tying up firewood. He then hog tied the man's hands to his ankles, tight and hard. The sand and gravel were soaking up the blood. He dragged him over to a tree and lashed him tightly to it.

The dogs kept lunging at him, snapping at a face he could no longer protect, and Matt called them off. They had done enough damage. They all stood a little way off, then sat down, panting and smiling, bloody mouthed, trembling and excited, wagging their tails and pleased with themselves, wanting the fun and excitement to continue. The biggest animals still had hackles raised and continued growling softly, their ears flattened, eagerly awaiting any signs of further action. Whenever the conscious man moaned, they would want to fly at him again.

The oldest female, Khanyi's loyal and close protector, was badly injured, whining and trying to reach around to lick her shoulder. She had been slashed with the cane knife, swung at her early on in the attack, and had a deep gaping wound in the muscle, almost to the bone. She was bleeding hard, crying and shaking away the blood. The adrenalin was keeping her on her feet, but the wound needed to be stitched.

Matt also began to shake. It had been so fast, so violent and so close. If Knox hadn't come when he had… The huge man walked over to the first man he had felled, stooped and turned him over roughly using his boots. 'Ah, this one is dead, Boss.' Then he went to see about the other tsotsi in the kitchen, now bleeding steadily from wounds in his chest and stomach, and gradually recovering from the blow to the head. He was sitting up looking dazed, still on the tiled floor.

Knox roughly grabbed one arm and dragged him over the kitchen floor and into the yard, dropping him there in the dirt. He was conscious and moaning, he was sorry, he was hungry, he just needed money. 'No more fighting, please no more fighting'.

Knox grabbed him by his neck, lifted him and dragged him further away from the house and onto the lawn, then threw him up against the tree, next to his partner, grabbing some rope from the garage and tying him to the trunk, tightly and painfully, with knots that could not be undone.

He made no effort to dress his wounds. Instead he began taunting him merrily. 'Woza umfaan, woza. I'm still hungry. I have only eaten one tonight, I want to take another one. One rubbish is not enough, my stick is still hungry to eat again'.

The man cried out, pleading, begging for them to call the police.

Knox swore at him, making that utterly insulting 'Ngxa!' noise you make from the side of your mouth, used only to demean a fool or berate idiocy. 'I must call the police for what? I'm going to teach you myself. The police will take a long time to come, and they know nothing. Maybe they will come too late for you.'

He stood in front of the man and began slowly and casually sharpening a long green stick with his small Okapi knife, deliberately letting the shavings fall onto him and occasionally testing the point. 'After I teach you, you Satan, you can't forget easily. You are going to remember tonight forever more.'

He was in his element, calmly terrifying the two survivors and repeatedly threatening them, waving the sharpened stick at their eyes, genitals and stomachs.

They moaned loudly.

Matt had never seen this brutal side to the quiet giant living among them, and came up behind him, walking painfully, still shocked, and asked quietly how he had realised what was happening.

Knox had been at home relaxing, listening to the radio. 'I heard the dogs, I'm thinking it's a problem when I hear the dogs making a big noise, then I heard you shouting so I came running quick quick. I was resting, listening the radio, getting ready to come for work.'

'You saved my life, Knox, and you saved Khanyi's as well.'

'Aah no, it's no problem,' the huge man replied. 'If I'm catch a rubbish like this, for sure I will beat them until dead. These other two are still lucky because I came late. In the house I never get chance to catch his head a straight shot, only to chase him, outside space is enough, I can beat them more easy. Now I am going to teach them something until tomorrow. They need to suffer.'

He paused. 'Can I beat them more, Boss? Just a little more? Make a small fire to teach them? You can go inside.'

Matt looked at his face and realised he was serious, but told him to stop. They had already killed an intruder that night, a fact that horrified him, but this seemed perfectly normal to the massive night watchman. But the shocking events of that evening had already gone further than anything Matt had ever experienced in his previous life.

He went inside and called the local police station, who predictably said they were facing a problem. 'Sorry, Mr Button, we are having shortage of transport,' but they thought they could maybe come in the morning. He then called the security force from the sugar estate who arrived within a few minutes, driving at great speed, two white vans roaring up the drive with orange flashing lights carrying several burly guards in khaki uniforms.

They were delighted to share in the excitement and merrily joined Knox, hurling cheerful insults at the two captured criminals, asking them questions, laughing as they handcuffed them to each other, and then chaining them to the inside of the van with a steel canopy and bars on the windows. They were not cruel to them, but were unsympathetic, manhandled them roughly into the vans, and then formally thanked the Barton household for catching them. The three were well-known, violent and dangerous, and had previously opened fire without hesitation on security and police in two different encounters.

The firearm was mentioned and then reluctantly recovered, much to Knox's disappointment.

The dead man's head was covered up with an old fertilizer sack. The dogs sniffed at his feet and hands as his body was dumped, without ceremony, onto the second open van, where he was laid out and then covered with an old dog's blanket.

A brief statement was taken from Matt and Knox then and there, written laboriously on the bonnet of the security van under the headlights. Khanyi had dressed his wound as best she could. Matt noticed that no effort was made to attend to the criminal's injuries, other than a brief examination and rough assessment. The security officers were far more concerned with the stab wound bleeding on his back, and the severely injured dog. They said they would arrange for a vet to come first thing in the morning, the same one who attended to their guard dogs.

They were as good as their word and she was duly stitched up the next day and would recover and survive, braver than ever.

Matt was the only driver at the homestead, but one of the officers went off into the darkness and roused Musa, who quickly drove Matt to a local industrial clinic that had a night nurse on duty. She phoned up the local medical officer on call, and while he was coming out she fussed over him, doing her best to cut away the cloth and thoroughly clean up and dress the deep wound. The doctor arrived, summoned from his bed, a surgical gown over his pyjamas, and he proceeded to flush out the wound with disinfectant and a flexible steel needle, an agonizing process, and then stitched him up under local anaesthetic, closing the mouth of the injury. It was deep and would be sore, but Matt was young and it would heal. The doctor administered some powerful pain killers and something stronger for the shock. Matt was drowsy and getting numb by the time they got back to the farm.

Knox remained at the house, always keeping very close to Khanyi who by now was badly shocked. He was uncharacteristically gentle, and surprised her by making her sit down and drink a big cup of sweet tea that he had prepared, covering her with a blanket and showing a tender side to his nature she had not seen before. He would not leave her alone until Matt returned, standing over her and watching her like a deeply comforting giant.

With his help, Khanyi had also done her best to clean up and dress the wounded dog and had given her some medication to make her sleep, but the animal was in great pain, whining, crying and still trying to reach her shoulder. They made a bed for her in the kitchen, a great treat for any of the dogs, and she settled.

Once Matt had returned, Knox left them huddled together in the fully lit house, and walked many times around the property, inside and outside the plot, searching for any more in the group that might be hiding in wait and hoping to flush another one out. He walked around quietly, playing his torch over the darkest areas and patrolling the fence line with the dogs keeping him company. There was nothing.

Eventually, late at night, they all slept, dogs and humans alike, all except for the tall looming presence of Knox, roaming around the garden with the animals, talking softly to them, praising their bravery, their bold hearts and their strong jaws, and singing old Zulu war songs quietly to himself. He was filled with an unholy joy about clubbing the thief who had died, the feel and the sweetness of the blow bringing back memories of another time.

Had he not told Boss Matt that thieves would come, and he would need protection?

Had he not protected him?

Was he not a man? He was a giant!

Was he not feared? He was feared!

Would the thieves not have killed Matt and raped Khanyisile?

Was he not a warrior?

It was an eminently satisfactory evening's work for him, doing what he loved to do, and he likened it to killing vermin.

The following day dawned and, despite their shock and Matt's injuries, the mood had lifted and their life gradually began to return to normal again, slowly resuming its peaceful steady rhythm after a few weeks of recovery.

It brought them closer together.

Chapter 31

For the first time in her young life, Khanyi felt truly cherished, and hesitatingly began spreading her wings, feeling a little more sure of herself. They had both recovered from the shock of the farm attack and now had the utmost trust in Knox, a devoted guard who would lay his life down for them. His tall and steady presence was reassuring.

They had added an electric fence around the property. She was learning different skills, and meeting new people daily, and found herself experiencing a whole range of unexpected and intense sensations.

She was feeling emotionally and physically thoroughly loved. She was proud to be with Matt, and felt almost a part of him. She had also subtly changed her style of dress, and unconsciously found in herself a newfound confidence to speak to people she didn't know, no longer fearful of white people or complete strangers. People somehow sensed that she had arrived.

After spending all her working life in domestic service, she was sensitive to an unspoken awareness that she was the same, but different. She was no longer regarded as a domestic worker. Somehow, subtly, her status had changed. People would ask her opinion on matters, and they had become friendlier, the only ones who really shunned her being some of the older white women, whose husbands worked in the sugar mill and on the estates.

A few of them had drawn their own bitter conclusions, and gossiped that as far as they were concerned, she was still 'that kitchen girl' who'd just happened to come up in the world by sleeping with her new boss, but she had very little contact with them, or the rumours they spread, and it seldom upset her unless they met them. No words were necessary, but she was sensitive to the dirty looks they gave her when she was with him. Matt never seemed to pick it up, but she felt it clearly although she rarely spoke of how it hurt.

He, by now, didn't even like to accept new work unless she was with him to help receive it. She was the person who most often answered incoming phone calls and she no longer felt nervous talking to the men who phoned in, even if they abruptly asked her complicated questions about when something would be ready, or demanded from her technical answers to things she didn't fully understand.

Often, having worked closely together for some time, she already knew the answer, and could tell them exactly when it would be ready, but even if she didn't know, she would calmly inform them that she would check with the workshops (as though it were a big place, with many people employed) and call them back. She enjoyed the sense of power and the separation that the phone gave her, and was learning many new phrases and expressions connected to the work they did.

People who didn't greet properly, no longer upset her as before. She would calmly make them wait for her to call them. She had learned not to drop everything she was doing, or rush and disturb Matt if he was in the middle of something, concentrating hard with his welding mask down. She had begun to understand just what intense concentration it took to produce the kind of workmanship he was known for, and she had also learnt that he could not stop and break a run of weld, without spoiling the finish. She was invariably polite and friendly on the phone, and kept herself informed about what stage different jobs were at, but no longer felt subservient to their customers. Knowing that Matt was around, and knowing that he always told her what was going on each day, made a huge difference to the way she saw the outside world. She knew in great detail what was going on in their thriving little business.

She began unconsciously to live in two worlds, the old world of the domestic, SisKhanyi, the Barton's devoted employee, with her widespread extended family and her deep love of the two children, and another, different young woman, a 'real somebody', the young Miss Khanyisile, Mr Barton's partner, running a small business with Matt. The old Khanyi and the new were like two different people. Revelling in her new found confidence, she would bravely speak to customers and friends alike and greet them properly, even if they were totally unknown to her, just to be friendly. She had even been brave enough to call up defaulting customers to politely remind them about making payments, the hardest conversations to have.

Khanyi had noticed a young couple who sometimes came to Joao Batiste's church, and thought to herself that the woman looked very pretty, but also very sad, as though she were carrying something painful inside. She was always very well dressed and beautifully made up, but the couple kept a bit to themselves, and didn't stay behind to chat over coffee after the services. She somehow looked very different to the other women who joined the gatherings under the tree, like someone coming straight from a big town. Her clothes were stylish, colourful and up to date, and she wore many different outfits.

Khanyi decided that she would speak to this young lady and try to befriend her, something she would have never dreamed of doing before her relationship with Matt. Something inside her was urging her to talk to the young white woman, even though she was a complete stranger. As she had explained earnestly to Matt, she looked like a quiet but nice somebody, but also very sad. She could never determine the age of white people, but she seemed to be young, like her, and didn't seem to know anyone.

The next time they happened to meet was at the local butchery. Matt had left Khanyi there to buy some meat for the house, while he filled the van with diesel and picked up various supplies needed for the workshop. The young girl actually started the conversation, and they began speaking together about the price of steak, two young women from very different backgrounds, thrown into a similar environment. The woman was commenting on how cheap it was, compared to South Africa. Khanyi thought it expensive!

Her name was Tarryn Bezuidenhout, and she was newly married. Her husband worked for a local fertiliser supply company. He was called Frikkie. She was from Bloemfontein, in the Free State. She had been born and grew up there, and she had no friends in the local area, apart from him. They had only been married for five months, and she was finding it very lonely living out in the bush, and she missed her family and friends terribly.

The local expatriate women were not very friendly towards her. They didn't like how she showed them up, how much of her tanned legs she showed, or the revealing, young looking clothes she wore. She was young and stylish, and didn't seem to fit into the area. Frik often worked long hours, and she hated the dull days spent alone, time hanging heavy on her hands. Her family refused to visit them. Her father would not allow his car to 'ride on a gravel road' in his words, so she could only see them when she visited Bloemfontein, but Frik was usually working weekends and it was hard to get away. She could drive herself, but was scared to drive such a long way on her own. They stayed in a farm cottage that his company rented, nothing like the homestead where Khanyi and Matt lived, much smaller. Khanyisile found out later, and it came as a surprise to her, that there were many white people living in houses far smaller than theirs, with small gardens and no vegetables grown.

Tarryn had a TV, but there was no movie house, nowhere to get her nails done, no clothing shops or hairdresser, and she could only get Swazi or Mozambican radio channels. Her old life, the clubbing at weekends, and her young, lively, funny Afrikaans student friends, were sorely missed. Very few of them ever made the effort to travel to Swaziland. She longed to go out for a drive, to go and pick up a cappuccino, or meet a friend for pizza or a movie, and she was becoming desperately lonely. She was a city girl. She knew very little about the hot lowveld, the poisonous snakes, growing sugar cane, or the country around her, and she was feeling very isolated. She was not permitted to work without a work permit in the kingdom, something that Khanyi had helped to arrange for Matt relatively easily.

She responded warmly to Khanyi's approach, and they arranged to meet at the Barton's for tea. This was a first for Khanyisile, playing the host and inviting someone to *her* house for a little social event. It felt very strange, playing the madam role, but she had watched and listened to Melanie doing it enough times to follow the process. She had always been the humble domestic worker in the background, preparing trays of coffee, tea and biscuits, politely placing them carefully on the coffee table when people visited, and going off to occupy the children, while the women chatted. Now she would be sitting comfortably and receiving a guest whom she had invited to their house, herself, for the first time ever.

After a slightly awkward start, the visit was a success. Tarryn had found her way to the Barton's farm without getting lost, but was then almost struck dumb by how grand it seemed compared to their little house. She had no experience of visiting a young black woman of her age, living in so much more affluent circumstances than her own. Khanyi slowly realised that, despite always looking beautiful and glamorous, she was quite shy, and keen to make friends. She asked question after question about her Swazi family, how she had met Matt (whom she had never met, but had heard about) and where Khanyi was from. She told her the whole story, fearing that it might change things between them, but she was honest, and Tarryn accepted their history without looking as surprised as she felt. She loved their courtship.

'My God,' she commented breathily, her long eyelashes fluttering dramatically over her big blue eyes, as she flicked her blonde tresses back, 'that's so romantic, Khanyisile!'

After chatting for some time, she innocently asked if Khanyi had been out with many other men before, and was amazed at her answer, widening her eyes again when she heard that she hadn't really had any proper boyfriends before. Tarryn's background was very different. She had been out with many young men when she was at varsity, but had found them a bit boring, mostly interested in cows, hunting or rugby, but she regretted never finishing what she was studying, instead leaving her studies and getting married to Frik.

She was actually the better educated of the two. He had started working straight after school. She, at least, had studied for nearly three years, and still wanted to finish her marketing degree. She loved animals. They had a tiny herd of dairy cows that they kept, selling the milk, and she was hoping one day to keep horses.

She lived for their monthly shopping trips to Nelspruit, when she could do some of the things she used to do, but they were the only highlight in her otherwise lonely life.

'Do you cook, Khanyi?'

Khanyi replied bashfully, 'Only a little bit. I am still learning. If it's many things at once, Matt helps me. I am not good in cooking.'

Tarryn told her, confidently and truthfully, that she was a very good cook, and suggested they bake some more involved dishes together. As they slowly became friends, she encouraged her new Swazi girlfriend to try out new dishes, and showed Khanyi how to follow a complicated recipe, gently explaining to her some of the processes she wasn't confident enough to follow. She had been to cooking classes and loved being able to show off one of her skills, after so many boring days spent alone in their cottage.

Khanyi was happy to introduce her to some of her local family and friends, really enjoyed spending time with her, and they began seeing each other regularly. Tarryn would deliver fresh milk to them in a plastic bucket, once a week. Matt liked it on his cornflakes. When the business was quiet, the two young women became a common sight, either Khanyi showing Tarryn around local markets, or Tarryn spending time with her in their kitchen. She had met Matt, and liked him, finding him friendly and down to earth, but his eyes only for Khanyisile.

Tarryn began driving out on occasional local outings, to visit at little homesteads in the bush with Khanyi, and she'd find herself sitting on a grass mat in a smoky hut, trying to chat to some people Khanyi knew in a stumbling and translated conversation, an experience unlike anything she had ever experienced before.

It opened her eyes to very different lives, and to the simple rural existence that surrounded them, and made her begin to see the very different meaning of family in Khanyi's culture. She was offered things to eat she had never tried before, and had many unexpected proposals of marriage from bold young men, fascinated by her delicate gold bracelets and earrings, who admired her long blonde hair and blue eyes, and liked to hear her accented voice. After only a brief greeting and impromptu discussion, they would propose marriage or request her love. These frequent proposals made them laugh together, and they became good friends. She was surprised to be so warmly welcomed into these traditional homes, and found that the reception she enjoyed was totally different to what she had been expecting, yet very much like the way Afrikaans people opened their homes to each other to 'kuier', to socialise and talk. The best foodstuffs and crockery would be brought out and used for tea.

Children (and occasional chickens and thin dogs), would wander in and out of these huts and listen to new conversations and the little ones would invariably be welcomed and hugged, hardly ever shooed away, regardless of what was being discussed. She found herself enjoying many warm hugs around the neck from snotty-nosed toddlers, who would simply walk towards her, and climb into her lap, or lean against her to stroke her hair, chatting away cheerfully, expecting her to understand every word. They would shyly stroke her golden skin, something new to touch.

Khanyi, as she spent more time with Tarryn, always such a smart looking young woman, was surprised to hear her talking openly about her personal difficulties, never thinking that whites even had such problems at home. She wasn't at all used to anyone discussing these things openly. Generally, it had always been expected of the women folk she knew to cope with challenges without complaining, and get on with life.

They felt their way towards each other, both learning and both open to new sensations. Tarryn now felt she knew someone well, and had made a new friend in a place in which she had felt so benighted. It began to make a huge difference to how she felt about living in the lowveld, and for a young, well brought up Afrikaans girl, it was also the first time she had grown emotionally close to a black African woman of similar age.

For Khanyi, their budding friendship had unconsciously lifted her personal status, and it subtly confirmed and empowered her own presence and self-belief. She somehow felt more valued and comfortable, even with someone apart from Matt, and the little confidences they shared helped her move beyond memories of her life as a domestic worker.

Tarryn just accepted her for what she was. She loved her ready laugh, her honesty and different expressions, and Khanyi was being influenced by her in small ways, once in a while being persuaded to try a little make up, or to look through the kind of magazines that she had never read, but remembered Melanie reading.

Khanyi had never felt before that she could offer valued advice and guidance to a white person apart from Matt and, as she helped Tarryn, she grew to love the sensation of a warm, close friendship, without demands.

In the months to come, Khanyi would shyly ask Tarryn one afternoon to help her arrange things for a special forthcoming event, as it seemed the natural choice, and Tarryn was deeply honoured and delighted to take on that special role.

Chapter 32

As word spread in the area, Matt began occasionally to receive repair work from a farm machinery workshop belonging to one of the big local estates, and gradually got to know one of the senior section managers, a Mr. Gabriel Dlamini. They first met when Gabriel brought his own small trailer to have its axle and frame welded before going on holiday. The little trailer, mainly used at weekends for firewood and water, and also loaded with luggage for longer holiday trips, had been grossly overloaded, many times over. Then it had broken its axle and he had been bluntly told it could not be repaired. Matt examined the weak, lightweight shaft, welded it and boxed it in, and welded again over the repair section, leaving it stronger than before, and then he rebuilt the frame and strengthened the floor, welding skilfully without blowing holes in the thin, lightweight materials. Then he painted over all the repairs. It was easy work for him.

Gabriel was both astonished and delighted. It was an affordable repair job, completed quickly, so that he could enjoy his holiday, and they became friendly from that day onwards.

Khanyi had often been visited by Gabriel, who had known Pat Barton and the family well, and he felt protective over her. Whenever the Bartons were away, he'd used to pass by from time to time, genuinely concerned to check if she was okay and that everything was alright at the house. He had told her many times when she was housesitting that, if there was any noise at night, she should phone him. If she needed transport anywhere, he would help. He used to make sure that even if they were away, anything they had paid for would still be delivered, so bags of coal would arrive and dustbins would be collected. He used his influence shamelessly, and looked after her like a younger niece.

He was a powerfully built African man, broad shouldered, tall but with a big stomach, a big booming voice and a bushy beard. He never spoke softly. His voice was always loud and his character was just as large. He was one of the well-known local characters, with many stories told about him in the area, and he had slowly forged a friendship with Matt over a period of time, always addressing Khanyisile with the utmost respect and often accepting her offer of tea. The couple had few close friends in the area, and Matt was glad to count Gabriel as one of them.

Gabriel was a devout believer, but not above using some very ripe and earthy language when he felt the situation warranted it. He usually went straight to the heart of the matter in a most unSwazi manner, but rarely failed to get his point across. He was warm and friendly, and Matt was receptive, and they had made a close connection strengthened over the passage of time, and through several visits and discussions. He had taught Matt a lot about the kingdom. Matt had repaired many farm implements for the estate.

Matt eventually felt he could talk to him about any Swazi matters, in a unique way.

One winter's morning, over a rusk and mug of steaming tea, Matt commented on the cold. Gabriel bellowed at him from deep within his immense brown parka jacket, smiling broadly,

'Aah, but Matt, for you Caucasians it's alright. You don't feel cold because you are having fur.'

Matt looked puzzled. 'We have fur?'

'Yebo!' Gabriel roared back at him, laughing at his confusion.

'Look at your legs and arms. You, you are having this fur, but we Swazis we don't have this, our skin is smooth, with no hairs. We Africans, we were made for hot places, whereas you Caucasians are made for the snow places, that's why God gave you fur.' He thought this was an immensely funny thing, and bent over, weakened by laughter until he wheezed and gasped for air at this essential difference between them.

'You see Matt, we Swazis are never supposed to stay in cold places, but you are supposed to stay there, so God has given you hairiness with fur on your skin to keep warm. We blacks, we don't like such cold places, so we don't need this fur.'

Matt chuckled, stroking his darkened jawline. He had grown to like Gabriel and was pleased that they could joke like this together. He shook his head at him, smiling back indulgently.

After several meetings, he began to know and respect Gabriel and became deeply fond of the honest and open man and his loud XXXL shirts and larger than life personality. One morning, Matt asked him for a private discussion, somewhere away from the house. Gabriel was immediately worried, thinking of possible trouble between him and Khanyisile. They drove off together, following each other, stopping and parking their vehicles on top of a nearby irrigation dam wall, standing together on the bank, looking over the still scene at the cool water moving quietly in front of them, lapping softly over the broad stone overflow.

Gabriel broke a small branch from a tree, as he always did, and began stripping away the leaves with his strong hands, looking away into the blue distance.

'Babe Gabriel', began Matt, 'I need to ask you about something...'

'There's no problem,' boomed the heavily built man in his deep voice, 'anything. What do you need my friend? I'm going to help you!'

Matt began stuttering. 'I'm not sure, I mean will it be… it's a bit difficult to explain.'

He looked down at the ground, 'I mean what would happen if we…'

He tried to start again.

Gabriel looked at him with what might have been a faint smile, suddenly feeling that he knew what was coming. He looked over his glasses at Matt, then removed his faded John Deere cap, and rubbed his head, covered now in short peppercorns of greying hair. He nodded his head briefly – go on what is it?

'Gabriel, well the thing is, I think I'm really in love with Khanyisile, but I don't know if I can, I mean what if we, what if we begin to erm, if we want to be together, are we doing anything wrong? Is it going to cause trouble? Will our friends like you be upset by us doing something like that, together?'

Gabriel looked at him as a father to a son, his deep brown eyes softening, then reached and grabbed Matt's left shoulder and right hand and squeezed them hard with his big hands.

'Hau, my friend there can be no problem. We here in the kingdom, we are very much used to this. If God never wanted some other races to marry the other ones, then why did he make so many colours? For what!

'Of course, some people will always make noise, but they are few and we, we who know you both, we know they are merely the foolish ones who like barking and making noise. If you feel love for this woman, then it's simple, you must be with her and she must know this.' He released Matt's shoulder and stood back, thinking, stroking his beard, then continued, 'Me, from my side I will be happy about this, because I know you are going to look after her, and I can see you make each other happy, even though you have got fur on your legs.' He chuckled again.

'She is still young, and you, you also are still very young. Of course I'm going to support you. Soon you will become one of us. I can see that she also loves you, and it's obvious that you also are very much interested to take her as a wife. This can also happen without any problem. I will even speak for you to her uncles because I know you as a proper somebody.'

A great weight lifted from Matt's shoulders, it was a blessing from someone he deeply respected.

'Thanks Gabriel,' he said bashfully. 'Thanks for what you said.'

'Aah, no its fine,' he replied. 'Fine. Anything else? Because I'm supposed to be at a section meeting at 10.30, and I seem to be running late.'

It was almost eleven.

He rushed off in a cloud of dust, driving down the bank and away in his 4 x 4, a bit too fast as always. Matt listened to the van revving high and disappearing into the distance, the dust left floating in the air, but felt the residual warmth left by their exchange. He relished the weight of approval it carried. He wanted to rush home and tell Khanyi that everything was going to be okay, because Gabriel had said so.

Strolling was one of the areas that Matt had had to be retrained for. The English like to go *for walks*. They leave at a pre-determined and specific time, regardless of rain, sleet or snow, and stride forth with a sense of purpose until they get to a certain place. They then stop, look at the view if it isn't completely obscured by clouds and rain, and sometimes take out their flasks to drink tea, or a little soup, have a final brief look around and promptly walk back. It is an activity with an end in sight, a healthy outdoor pursuit, an event with a distinct beginning and an end.

The Swazi people, he found, only do this kind of walk when they are going to work. Walking in Swaziland was usually more of a social event. Khanyi would walk in a series of zig zags, aimlessly crossing from one side of the road to the other, sometimes forwards, at other times walking backwards and facing him and always chatting. Walks were slow. She would hold his hand and tell him about funny events, funny things people had said, and stories she had heard. She would stop and pick some small flowers or a juicy stalk of grass, or point out butterflies, lovely clouds on the horizon or small birds. They would often come to a complete stop to greet people heading the other way, if she knew them at all, and she knew many.

When they went for a walk they seldom got to anywhere particular. Much walking around was done, but often very little actual distance would be covered. Sometimes they would venture as far as a local irrigation canal, or nearby dams, but he noticed she disliked being too close to big trees. She always said she feared the army caterpillars, but didn't know the words to explain not wanting to lurk under shadowy trees.

The Barton dogs loved this activity anyway, the longer the better, and would go leaping away in a random series of wide, joyful loops, often disappearing for long periods, then barking gleefully in the tall cane to the accompaniment of a great rustling and crashing whenever they put up guinea fowl or disturbed a cane rat. Sometimes they would catch one, emerging with the creature in their jaws, looking strangely puzzled at their success.

They would pop back out of the dense green cane, either far ahead of them, or sometimes far behind, and then run joyfully up to the couple like they had forgotten all about them and were surprised and delighted to unexpectedly find them there. The sharp cane leaves sometimes cut the edges of their eyes, but this never prevented them from exploring. It wasn't the kind of walk that Matt remembered, but was supremely relaxing, and utterly without purpose. It was a social event between them and a chance for him to look at his beloved Khanyi as she talked animatedly about all sorts of things and chatted away to him. He grew to love these 'walks'. In another world they would be called 'quality time'.

Not long after Matt's discussion with Gabriel, coming to the end of such a random walk late one afternoon, with shadows already lengthening, after strolling together for a long time in the deep green cane fields, he formally proposed to Khanyisile. They kissed, they hugged, and she wept with joy, accepting him immediately.

Six months later they had a large, colourful, musical, chaotic wedding, with elements of both cultures represented. There was much traditional dancing, with Khanyi in the middle of the front line, leading the dance, but the wedding itself was both European and

Christian, with Joao Batiste presiding over the ceremony, conducted in their garden.

Guests of honour included Amos from the stores, and their new friends, Frik and Tarryn. Salikh had even been invited from the UK, but did not come. Mr. Pearson sent them both an affectionate telegram message and transferred a generous wedding gift to them of one thousand British pounds. Shamrock Farms were represented by Paidric O'Connor himself, Kaitleen, her sister and two of her school friends. Paidric gave them a bottle of rare fifteen-year-old Irish whiskey and a perfectly cured Nguni cowhide. Many of their customers came too, and were lavish with gifts of blankets, cooking utensils, food stuffs and cash.

Tarryn was maid of honour and had taken the role seriously, proving to be a supreme organiser. She had loved doing nails and make up for the bride.

Teresinha sang beautifully, directing to them both a song she had chosen specially for the couple. It was a piece they both liked, a song about true love running deep and lasting eternally, and many guests were moved to tears. Matt though, was almost unable to take his eyes off Khanyi. She shone like her name.

She was wearing her full traditional attire for a wedding, and danced and sang beguilingly and gracefully, showing off rather more of her than he usually got to see in daylight, and dancing barefoot on the grass lawn, white bracelets of tiny cowrie shells around her slender ankles. She had never looked happier and her flashing smile and sparkling eyes were utterly entrancing. He could hardly take his eyes off her. As she danced, guests would run up to her and cover her shoulders in luxurious deep blankets. When there were too many, one of the elder females would dance up to her and remove them, folding them neatly and setting them aside, valued traditional gifts from the visitors. The pile grew quickly. Blankets were the favoured gift.

The tables were bedecked in Swazi traditional cloths, and long white sheets of material had been hung between the low boughs of trees for shade, with tables and chairs set beneath them. A number of aunties had emerged mysteriously, coming from all over the country in the days beforehand to help with the cooking and serving, all of whom were now extended family.

Matt had actually played very little part in the arrangements, but just took it all in, feeling honoured and amazed by all the arrangements, the singing, the celebrations and the dancing.

There were a number of speeches, often given by scruffy and grizzled elders that Khanyi said she hardly knew, some of whom she thought had gatecrashed. They were not even invited, and often went on rather too long, but it didn't matter. The translations were usually much shorter than the original rambling speech.

There was also an extraordinary impromptu speech from Gabriel Dlamini, who had stood in place of her father, by now too old to travel, and he was very funny. He had already played a crucial role in negotiating the price of the lobola cattle, sorting out catering, security, parking guards, portable toilets, music and a great many other arrangements. He handled all of these matters with dignity and a lot of personal influence.

He proved to be a surprisingly gifted and confident public speaker, and told everyone of the time Matt had asked him for advice. He tried to imitate his British accent, and although he did so very badly, he nonetheless somehow managed to put across something of his nervousness and the sincerity of the event. Khanyi had never heard the story before and loved it, laughing until she had to wipe tears from her eyes.

A beast had been slaughtered and prepared and a great deal of meat was eaten, over several hours of happy feasting, and Matt then had to remove his suit and change into traditional Invunulo, and it was time to step up, surrounded by throngs of new Bosibali and

Bomalume, brothers, brothers-in-law and uncles, to dance Bayagiya with them, as the successful young suitor.

Luckily, he had been coached beforehand by Musa, who'd given him secret lessons in a clearing deep in the cane fields for a few weeks, and he knew most of the steps, even the songs, stamping and moving fervently in the dust, so he did not make a complete fool of himself, more or less keeping the beat with his new 'brothers' to the deep voice of the sighubu drums, although he was really no dancer. To his surprise, and helped a little by a few drinks, he found that he actually enjoyed the dancing, even though everyone would shriek with laughter when he fell out of time. His bold efforts met with widespread approval.

The men's dances were spirited and prolonged. From time to time the warrior blood would run hot, and one of the guests would be so overcome with emotion they would leap to their feet, flinging aside their shoes, jacket and tie to cavort in front of him, seemingly highly threatening, waving a shield and a borrowed spear or sizeze, the short axe, shouting and calling and twirling and stamping under the trees in a solo dance of appreciation and support until they could dance no more, when they would finally twirl, overbalance and fall onto the dust, suited pants or not. Khanyi told him they were singing praises to him and to his family.

Frikkie and Tarryn, and the other white visitors, soon realised around lunch time, after the main event had started almost two hours after its planned start, that being concerned about timing was largely pointless. Nothing really followed the timetable, and nothing would, but Matt enjoyed his wedding all the more for this, just letting the loosely organised chaos wash over him in a joyous wave of colour, happiness, cultural pride, feasting and music.

Gabriel, Amos and several other Swazi friends and customers, including many of the Sibandze clan, all came in traditional attire, and in their numbers, with long colourful necklaces dangling from right shoulder to waist, their stomachs, legs and chests exposed. Matt was surprised to see how pale their natural skin was under their shirts and pants, in some cases their necks and arms bearing tan lines just as evident as his own.

They all knew the ancient dances and songs, and the singing stirred their blood, made them feel young again and reminded them of their tribal history. They would join in, sing and dance for some time, then take their seats again, or fall to the grass and rest, even sleeping under the shady trees. It was a joyous, blessed, memorable and unique event that people spoke about for many years after.

Chapter 33

KHANYISILE WAS ALREADY A BEAUTIFUL and gracious woman, but had started to reveal something else. A certain, hard to define presence, seen sometimes in a woman who is deeply loved and well cared for. She had become more confident and poised, less easily thrown by unpleasant people or unexpected events.

Gradually, the healing passage of time had eroded their saddest memories, replacing them with new ones that they had made and shared together. Business episodes that had gone well, people they had known slightly, who had gradually became true friends. They forged a life together, with Khanyi still deeply-rooted in her country and her people, but equally devoted to their new life together, and Matt, slowly adapting, changing and becoming a little less intense, less driven, more at ease with himself and his work, and more relaxed.

He barely thought now about his previous life, stepping on and off endless aircraft, in and out of strange towns and airports, and constantly on the move. Occasionally, they would take a drive and go out for a dinner together, but there was something different in her now, that exuded confidence, a subtle change about her persona, invisible yet clearly evident.

There was also something apparent in their relationship, a oneness, a melding of souls that had created an underlying strength and combined character that made them greater together than either of them could ever be apart. No waitress would ever dream of speaking insultingly to Khanyi now. They somehow displayed a warmth between them that few couples have, a deep unspoken bond between them that had been tested and survived.

When anyone caused harm or upset to one of them, they would quickly find that they had also harmed the other, and in turn might have offended a surprisingly large family, and this closeness to each other became a talking point in the area. They were popular, and had become a young couple who would get invited to occasional parties, those hosted by other likeminded people, who no longer saw race as an issue in determining who can properly be asked to dinner.

Khanyi started learning to drive, and was proving terribly bad at this, but was determined to master it as it would give her greater independence.

When their first child was born, she was named Mpumelelo Jacqueline Barton, but called Pumi or PJ for short, and she was growing up with two loving parents, a little girl blissfully unaware that her parents had been brought together by tragic circumstances.

Khanyi would often be seen walking slowly along in the area, close to their home, sporting a big white sunhat and a sun dress, showing off her slender shoulders and arms, pushing along a stunningly beautiful little honey-coloured girl in an old fashioned pram, a child blessed with golden brown hair, and strangely dark emerald green eyes, who chattered away in a mixture of baby talk, siSwati and English, but with a very faint North of England accent. Matt would occasionally be strolling beside them.

Five dogs of different sizes would be seen following them along the dirt roads between the massive green stands of lush sugar cane, always sniffing and alert for opportunities, guinea fowls to catch, irrigators to bark at, and leguaans to chase, and at certain times there was the unique smell of feathery sugar cane flowers swaying lightly and delicately in the air.

Their home was busy, and sometimes noisy. There was often machinery grinding and cutting outside, while visitors chatted away inside, and there were several fierce dogs roaming around. The Bartons eventually employed a nanny themselves, a quietly respectful young woman from Hhohho district who only ever spoke SiSwati to Pumi, and helped Khanyi with the housework. She doted on the little girl and was teaching her the deep, pure form of unadulterated SiSwati only heard in the rural areas.

Khanyisile could feel inside her that there was another little one on the way, and knew from three secret Swazi beliefs, and from her body and her ancestors, that it was certain to be a little boy, a son who would look like Matt and grow up to take loving care of his sister. She and her husband were unusually happy with each other, and their way of life. It no longer mattered what happened elsewhere, they had made a new life from the loss of the old ones.

Chapter 34

It was a lazy Sunday afternoon in early September and nearly four years had passed since Matt's return from England and his homecoming. Joao Batiste and Teresinha were visiting their close friends, Khanyi and Matt, and the two couples were sitting chatting in the garden, listening to the wood pigeons and guinea fowls competing, providing a free bushveld musical background to conversation after a relaxed lunch together.

Joao and Teresinha were visiting for a reason. They were keen to invite their young friends, the Bartons, to join them for a short holiday in the far north of Mozambique, driving up to a remote area of beach close to the place where they had first met. It was a significant wedding anniversary for the Dos Santos, and they were both longing to be back near the sea, feeling the warmth, and briny touch of the Indian Ocean breezes they remembered so well, and drawing spiritual strength from the feeling that comes from being close to the ever changing light.

Teresinha's family had a small beach house, a Casa de Praia on the coast, and Joao was feeling emotionally weary, in need of new spiritual inspiration, a break from preaching, and wanting to put some distance between himself and other people's troubles.

Teresinhsa, while she wanted to see her own family again, also wanted a chance to show Khanyisile where she had grown up and where her real home was, the two women also having become close friends.

They agreed to pack and prepare two vehicles for the journey, to plan and buy the necessary foodstuffs for the holiday and make their way in convoy to the far north, negotiating as they travelled the numerous, and often corrupt, roadblocks. For this they relied on an unstoppable blend of Joao's knowledge of the area, their faith in divine influence, the unspoken assistance of Theresinha's undeniable beauty and charm, all coupled to fluency in the local language and customs.

The holiday took some time to arrange. Matt had to clear his calendar and warn his key clients that he would be away for some time, Khanyi needed to arrange for someone to care for the house and dogs, feed the fowls and watch over the homestead. She also needed to pack extensively for Pumi Jacqueline, the little girl's luggage requirements far exceeding that of both her parents, and she needed to plan ahead for the catering and camping out. She had never done this before.

It was to be her first proper holiday, a real trip out of the Kingdom with the sole purpose of enjoying a time of rest, sunshine and idle leisure, and it would also be her first time to ever see the sea. In absolute secrecy she and her friend had driven to town one day and she'd bought a revealing and very daring ice white bikini, mostly at Tereshina's urging. She looked devastating in it, barely covering the essentials, and she was not sure if she was going to be brave enough to reveal so much of herself and her figure – far more than anyone other than her husband normally got to see. She also had no desire to get it wet at any point.

Khanyi could not swim, and had no intention of learning to. She would sometimes edge warily into the shallow end of a swimming pool if no one was around, and walk gently around, pushing slowly at the water before her, but she didn't like to be splashed and would never get her head wet. She could sort of doggy paddle and float.

She was quite scared of big surf, and utterly convinced that the ocean was filled with hungry and dangerous sea creatures. She imagined fearful looking things floating ominously in the bottomless darkness, circling in wait, ever hungry, preparing to bite and eat her immediately, or drag her into the cold depths if she ventured into their world.

She shyly shared these fears with Matt, who tried to reassure her that it would be a safe, sloping beach, but nothing that he or their friends said would change her mind. She was still excited about the trip though, looking forward to seeing the beach, and finding out what it was like, but only planning to view the sea from the safety of the shoreline. She had once asked Frikkie and Tarryn to tell her about the ocean but, although they had explained, it was hard for her to imagine a body of water that could run from one horizon to the other. How could there be that much water in one place? Let alone water that was filled with salt and always moving! She was excited to see it.

Of the four of them, she was the least affected by heat, and was seldom troubled by it. She somehow seemed to remain cool even on the hottest of days, but where they were travelling it was going to be hot, with a long, badly rutted road lying between them and their holiday.

The journey took two entire days, but they eventually reached their destination safely, having had a simple passage through most of the roadblocks by refusing resolutely to pay bribes en route, but occasionally offering the soldiers a friendly cold drink. They had encountered serious trouble only once, at an arbitrary check point positioned randomly somewhere north of Xai Xai.

At this check point, where both vehicles were forced to park and wait out on the hot tarmac, an 'officer' eventually sauntered out from under a tree in civvies and an assortment of military medals, a heavily rusted AK47 slung loosely over one shoulder. He rudely and abruptly confiscated their documents for 'inspection', and then tried to extract a hundred US dollars from Matt, who had driven up to the barrier wearing sunglasses. The fine was for wearing sunglasses when it was partially cloudy, as the wearing of them was therefore legally unnecessary, and this, as such, constituted a crime that would evidently endanger all other Mozambican road users. He demanded this payment using tactics that usually worked with foreigners, and began shouting in Portuguese, waving the automatic rifle around with increasing agitation, sometimes pointing it close to them. The heat of the day, not being allowed out of the car and their tiredness worsened things, and the argument had continued for some time and became heated. Pumi began to cry, upset by the noise and wailed loudly in her baby seat.

The official was slowly realising that these were not just naïve tourists who would cave in easily, and had just changed to the final stages of his extortion attempts, wheedling and whining and complaining that he needed something '*to help him to remember them*', asking outright for a slightly lesser financial gift, as this might make it easier to let them off the fine for Matt's grave offence.

At this point, Joao, his Mediterranean temper and blood now fully fired up, walked purposefully back from his vehicle, parked in front, and asked in rapid Portuguese for a written copy of the fine. The official sneered at him, warning him, gesturing towards him with the gun and directing him back to his car or face arrest. Joao coolly said he would need to discuss the fine with the state prosecutor, who happened to be a close personal friend of his. They were all due to attend dinner with him at his residence that night, as a party of guests from Swaziland, and they were now going to be arriving very late, owing to the actions of this officer. As the sunglasses offence was so serious and important, he merely wished to explain their delay to the prosecutor, when they met. They would obviously require the fine to show their friend, when he apologised for their rudeness, for spoiling the dinner and their unexplained late arrival.

Joao did actually know the prosecutor. He had responded to an altar call one emotional evening many years back, and the prosecutor had confessed to a long standing affair with his secretary, but the dinner date was somewhat extemporized. The intervention, however, had an instant effect.

On receipt of the news, a sudden and startling transformation came over the police official, who instantly concluded that, despite their wrong doings, he was prepared to overlook the offence and had decided that there was no pressing reason to further delay the holiday makers. He instantly returned the three passports, gave back the offending sunglasses that he had been 'testing', and handed back their vehicle documents, and even half-heartedly began to repack their unloaded luggage, which the soldiers had been stripping for valuables. Then he thanked them for visiting him, saluted them, and wished them well on their way.

The reaction to the name of the Prosecutor was so remarkable that in a final flourish, with a beaming smile, he expressed hopes that they would have a safe journey and formally welcomed them and wished them a wonderful holiday in Mozambique. Khanyisile had much to say about the unnecessary delay and the Shangaan Police, very little of it complimentary.

When they had started driving again and calmed down, Matt remembered seeing a similar remarkable change come over an unpleasant official once before, and told Khanyi about an incident in Nigeria when, after having had all of his welding equipment confiscated as Western spying equipment, he had casually mentioned the name of a Nigerian oil billionaire to the 'Captain' of the informal roadblock. The same chief, businessman and politician whose refinery plant he was supposed to be repairing. Everything was suddenly released and given back to him, and he was given an armed escort to the business at high speed, and left in peace to complete his repairs.

The lengthy obstruction finally out of the way, they resumed their long drive and eventually reached their destination, fed up of bouncing around on dusty roads, with a tired, now hungry and fractious child. They unloaded their belongings, helped by various kindly staff who seemed to appear from nowhere, explored their rooms and settled into a simple but comfortable beach house, set back from the shoreline in a stand of tall palm trees, with the sound of the waves breaking gently on the shore, about fifty metres away. It had a large, shady verandah facing the coastline, and as soon as they sat down, sinking deeply into the old hardwood couches, strewn about with soft cushions, and had quenched their thirst with some ice cold drinks, they began to feel the dust, stress and heat of the journey falling away from them, and a wonderful lassitude settling over them.

Four days later, Khanyi was strolling along the beach, barefoot, wearing her now famous bikini, covered from the hips down in a sarong for modesty. Pumi was being cared for by the doting Dos Santos couple, paddling safely in a rock pool and finding endless treasures and shiny stones, and gravely presenting these priceless gifts to each adult in succession. Matt meanwhile was snorkelling in the shallows and looking at tiny tropical fish.

Khanyi had become brave enough to walk along the surf line, as it broke along the flat beach, her ankles periodically being splashed and gently soaked by the waves as they petered out, before turning to begin their endless journeying once again.

She had gone for a short walk as the heat of the day left the coastline. It was late, and long shadows cast over the scene, subtly altering the colours of the sea, rocks and sand. Walking slowly along, she noticed in the distance, further up the beach, something tumbling over and over in the surf.

She thought it was a small sea creature of some kind, or a turtle, but the way it tumbled over and over without resistance meant it must be dead and safe to approach. She kept watching, so as not to lose sight of it and walked more purposefully towards it, now quite a distance from the others, inquisitive and quite intrigued as to what it might be.

Something seemed to slide across her soul and she sensed a sudden chill, as if a cool breath of air had blown across her lightly clothed body, touching her bare shoulders, midriff and legs. It was a feeling she had last felt when she saw the owl, and yet this was somehow different, and she inhaled suddenly, taking a sharp audible breath as the intensity of the feeling rushed over her soul.

Close to it now, she timed her move and waited as it was swept out, and then jogged down into the low waves to meet it as it washed in again, now able to see it more clearly. It looked like a toy, like a child's soft toy of some kind. It was not a jellyfish or a crab, a dead fish or a coconut. She reached down swiftly, and lifted it out of the sea, shaking off a strand of seaweed, and some of the sand it had accumulated, rolling over and over in the surf.

It was a golden teddy bear, a little child's bear about the size of a large doll. It had been in the sea for a long time, the fur on its back and limbs had become light green and slimy, and there was even some algae on the bottom of its paws. But it was intact, with two warm brown eyes that had been gazing upwards into the African sky for ages.

Khanyisile felt as though her feet were sinking into the earth. As though the world had changed somehow, shifting on its axis, and was now turning around her, spinning in an odd, unaccustomed direction and making her dizzy. She felt her body becoming immensely heavy and felt faint. There was a presence, a certain atmosphere attached to this thing in her hands that she remembered from a life she had lived previously. She knew it, she had seen it before somewhere, seen it many times, clutched tightly by some small child.

With shaking hands, she lifted it closer to her face and gently turned back the little bear's right ear. There, faintly written into the fabric of the soft cloth, but still distinct and clear, were two names written in a rounded girlish handwriting, faded with time, one word set under the other for all time:

Jackie
Barton

Khanyi felt weak, she could no longer breathe, and collapsed onto her knees in the warm sea, clutching the little wet bear to her chest and sobbing out loud. This was her little one's special teddy bear. She would never go to sleep without it. She took it with her everywhere. Khanyi had been asked to attend many tea parties in the garden with this bear, pouring brown tea made from mud and water into tiny cups, and feeding it jelly tots and leaves.

Her own little one had been holding this bear when her life had come to an end, and the ancestors had made her meet Matt, fall in love with him, marry him and come to this place for a holiday, waiting until today before letting the bear wash onto the shore, then making her walk along the coast at the right time and find it in the sea. Soaking wet, sandy and salt stained, she hugged it tightly to her breasts, her hands shaking, squeezing it, and holding it like a priceless family heirloom.

Tears welled up in her eyes as she knelt and bent over the little bear, and she lowered her head and wept, a great keening cry coming from her very soul, letting out all the years of her pain and loss.

Teresinha and Joao heard something untoward in the distance, a cry sounding above the sound of the sea, and looked up, only seeing her from a distance. She had apparently fallen into the surf or was hurt. In a panic, and knowing she could not swim, Joao immediately threw down his straw hat and dropped the handful of treasures Pumi had given him to hold, and began sprinting along the beach, towards her.

'Watch the baby, Minha Querida,' he shouted. 'Khanyi has fallen! Something is wrong.'

He ran up to her, his footprints deep in the wet sand, but she was already recovering shakily from the great shock and was upright again, stumbling out of the surf and into the afternoon shadows, pale faced and wide eyed, her delicate sarong now all wet and sandy. She was clutching something dirty and wet in her arms.

'Joao!' she called. 'Joao, look I have found something from Jackie! I find it in the sea!'

He came up to her and hugged her tightly, feeling her heart pounding in her chest, her breathing very fast.

'Look Joao,' she gasped. 'Look what it says! I know this bear! It is Jackie's bear, it is her bear. It's the toy of my little one. My little girl who is gone. It has been in the sea all this time, floating, coming here to find me. This is hers; she was holding it on the aeroplane. She was touching this. She was with it right at the end! This was part of my family!'

He nodded, confused but letting her carry on

'I know it very well, this little bear!'

She was sobbing, tearful and gasping for breath, but carefully showed him the name written into the ear, faded but clearly legible.

Joao read the name and clutched her tightly, gripped like her by strong emotions. He had not known the Barton family himself, but he knew what they meant to her, and knew she had loved them devotedly.

'This is a divine blessing, Khanyi. It is a blessing straight from God and from the saints. Is a complete miracle. You were the one He chose to find this bear, because He knows how much you loved your children, how much love you had for the little Jackie, meo amore.' He too was overcome then and, wiping tears from his eyes, he began speaking with great passion, praying aloud, thanking God for the bear, blessing Khanyisile and her deep love for her family, a love still strong and undiminished after all this time.

He thanked the Almighty for making the currents and the waves, the wind and the storms. He could no longer express his emotions in English, they had become too strong, and he broke into fervent and rapid Portuguese, raising his eyes and hands to the heavens and praying aloud, lifting and kissing the cross strung round his strong neck.

Khanyi brought him back to where they were standing together, getting wet in the rising tide. 'Joao, we must find Matt, I must show him'.

He hugged the young woman tightly to him, and they set off together, arms around each other's waists, moving back down the beach towards Pumi and Teresinha.

Teresinha had run into the foam and had managed to summon Matt out of the sea, and he already knew something had happened. He was sitting down in the surf in the distance, removing his mask and flippers, then he threw them high up onto the sand and came running toward them both. He came up to them breathless, his chest heaving, still dripping with sea water, shaking his head and wiping drops out of his eyes.

'Are you alright, Khanyi love? Did something sting you?'

Khanyi fell into his arms, flung her arms around him and wept. It took several minutes before either she or Joao could gather themselves and she could explain what she had found.

As Matt turned over the fragment of cloth and read the name, he remembered his niece sitting in his house with the little bear, how she had to have it sitting with them at the supper table, how it would be put down to sleep with them both each night and had its own miniature blue dinner jacket and pyjamas. How he had seen them off at the airport with the bear in Jackie's hands.

It was a well-loved and much travelled little bear, never out of her sight.

He slowly collapsed onto the warm sand, gazing at the little creature held in his hands.

'This is amazing, Khanyi love. This is the most amazing thing I have ever seen. It's unbelievable! She must have had it with her when… she must have been holding it as, when they, when the plane…' Overcome by the memories, he too was unable to continue and the two of them sat together, hugging each other and crying.

Joao was banging away at his back and shoulders with his big strong hands. 'Is a miracle, Matt! Is really a miracle, is really something incredible from God, like Jonah spit out from the whale. Never in my life have I heard of this.'

Khanyi had tears in her eyes, but was smiling through them and wiping them away. Her heart felt hugely lightened. 'She was with him, Matt. My little girl was not alone.'

She paused, catching her breath and collecting herself. 'Jackie was holding him. Now he is with me, and she too is with me. I can never leave this bear alone, never again.'

She never did.

There was nothing to bury, there were never any other remains found, but the beloved bear travelled with them back to their home and had pride of place in their bedroom for the remainder of their lives together. The homecoming was completed.

Printed in Great Britain
by Amazon